THE WITCH OF FERATHAN

An Aepistelle Chronicles Novella

RYAN HOYT

Machete & Quill Press

PRÈFACE

This novella takes place seventy years before the events of *Gemma Calvertson and the Forest of Despair*. No prior knowledge of the world of Aepistelle is required to enjoy this story. You may read them in any order you choose.

The first chapter of *The Forest of Despair* follows this story for your enjoyment. Thank you for reading.

Drops of water plummeted into an unseen puddle in a natural rhythm. The only other sounds to shatter the heavy silence of the cave were the rapid breaths and wheezes of a man. He struggled to control himself, to inhale and exhale slowly, to quiet himself in the pitch-black, claustrophobic hellhole he frantically wandered. He leaned against a frigid, rounded wall and closed his eyes, though it was no darker behind the veil of his eyelids than it was in the earthen tomb that enveloped him. He jabbed his left thumb into his right hand, pressing on the webbing between his thumb and pointer finger. After what must have been seconds but felt like minutes, he regained his composure. He slowed his breathing. The wheezing faded.

He knelt down, but his knees buckled. He

relented, allowing himself to sit, the seat of his pants absorbing the puddle in which he now rested. Had he been born in the southern lands of the Aepistelle continent, he would have prayed for protection from one of the many gods worshiped by the people there. He was from Ferathan, though, and his people didn't practice religion. They didn't look to deities in an invisible realm for hope or courage. They didn't rely on prayers or ancestral dances for a productive harvest season or protection from evil.

Gaethen Devorac sat and focused on controlling his breathing, a necessity since his early childhood, thanks to the affliction in his lungs. With his eyes closed and his breaths coming slower, Gaethen found himself drifting off into unexpected sleep. It may have been five minutes or five hours before he shook himself back into consciousness. All he knew was darkness, and that wouldn't change until he found his way back out of this place.

With a deep breath, Gaethen stood. The numbness that had seized his legs on that wet, rocky floor made it difficult to walk, but he persisted. He kept his left hand in contact with the wall of the cave and his right hand outstretched to make sure he did not crash into any unseen protrusion. He hoped he was moving in the right direction—he thought he remembered lowering himself down the slope he was now climbing. After several more minutes, he recognized a different quality to the air and was sure he was heading toward the mouth of the cave. However, his new confidence was nearly his undoing.

Gaethen sped up, lowering his left hand from the wall that guided him. He smiled; he was not going to die deep in the earth under the forest that lined the outskirts of his family's farm. He nearly enjoyed the sound of his boots clattering at a rapid clip against the wet floor of the cave.

That is, until he took a step that made no sound. Until his right boot did not make contact with the rock below him. Until he found himself flailing and falling down into an unseen pit.

Gaethen reached out, grabbing on to the jagged wall of the pit. By some chance—he and his people would not have called it a blessing, for that would imply it was the will of a god—he managed to catch himself. He clung to the rough stone wall for dear life, ignoring the warm blood that dripped down his hands and wrists, until his left foot found a divot just large enough to put some weight on, relieving some of the pressure on his palms. He began to wheeze again. He remained there, head bowed, as he forced himself to control his breathing once more and stop the sound that emanated from the depths of his chest.

As he hung there in the darkness, he suddenly heard a crunching sound, followed by pebbles pelting down on him from above. His first thought was that the wall of the pit was collapsing under his weight, that he was going to fall to his death at only twenty-four years of age. Then he heard what sounded like someone dropping down onto their belly up at the mouth of the pit.

"Just hang on, I'll help you," a voice said from above.

Had he imagined it? Surely, nobody from town or the neighboring farms would have known to come out and look for him here. He had no laborers of his own anymore and no surviving family back at his comfortably sized home next to a decaying barn. He was alone out here.

"Can you reach up with your hand? I think I can pull you up." It was a woman's voice. He thought again of his neighbors, the women and daughters of the nearby farms, but this voice did not sound familiar. There was a bit of an accent, one that didn't sound Ferathani.

"Who ... who are you?" Gaethen croaked in fear, his voice coming out shakier than he had expected. "Are you a forest nymph? A witch?" For generations, the Ferathani had passed down stories of creatures in the neighboring Forest of Despair—wickedness in the form of attractive women who would lure young men into the thick trees, then transform into beasts and attack their victims, eating all but their hands, which they left behind for their kinsmen to find. Even though his farm was at the edge of the forest, Gaethen avoided crossing the border whenever possible. Only a small handful of folks from Ferathan braved the forest with any regularity, usually traders on their way south to the Aepistelle kingdoms for commerce, or hunters and trappers who were after the game that thrived in the area. Gaethen had only gone in to look for his missing herd of sheep, and look where it had gotten him.

"Are you really in a position to be picky about who saves you?" A good-natured laugh came from above. "I can go away, if you think someone else will be along any minute to find you here. Or you can grab my hand. The choice is yours."

Gaethen let out a nervous laugh. The woman was right. She was his only hope of getting out of this cave alive.

"Okay, you're right," he said.

He took another deep breath, slightly bent his one stationary leg, then thrust his body upward, right hand outstretched. As it left the rock he was gripping, Gaethen felt the shredded skin on that palm, which he could only hope would be able to grasp his rescuer's hand strongly enough. He felt her warm skin as his fingers met hers. The woman reached down farther, closing her hand around his wrist, and he clasped hers in return. He squeezed tight in spite of the pain. With his right foot, he managed to find a knot of rock to push up on, and his left leg abandoned the safety of its own little ledge. With this new leverage and the surprising strength of the woman, he was able to grab hold of the edge of the pit with his left hand. His unseen savior pulled him the rest of the way up to safety. He sprawled, belly down, on the hard but welcoming floor of the cave. Without meaning to, he closed his eyes and fell into unconsciousness.

At some point, as he was being carried out into the open air and through the forest, Gaethen opened his eyes. He got two fleeting glimpses of his rescuer before he was pulled back into the darkness of slumber. When he woke in his own bed some time later, he wasn't sure if he had dreamed the face he had seen.

No, the *faces* he had seen.

At first, in the midnight shadows of the forest canopy, he had glimpsed an old hag's face surrounded by thin wisps of white hair. Then, as the moonlight shone through a gap in the trees, he had witnessed—on the same woman—the most strikingly angelic face and flowing red hair he had ever laid eyes upon.

She had been pure perfection.

CHAPTER 2

A pounding at the door dragged Gaethen into consciousness once again. He was sure there were no bills due, and he had not sent out collections notices to any of the farm's clients in three or four weeks. That left just one option for who would be calling on him: Jermaine Fielder.

Gaethen wavered a bit as he took his first steps out of bed. His legs felt like rubber, as if he hadn't walked in days. He reached for the wall to steady himself and made his way down the hall to the front door.

"You look like bloody hell," Jermaine said. He pushed past Gaethen and let himself inside. Behind him was his sister, Sana. "Well, it appears nobody ransacked the place, so maybe you weren't attacked. The bandages on your hands indicate that someone helped you—they look too neat for a man with two injured hands to have done himself. Who is the lovely lady?"

"Lady?" Gaethen asked. His mind was still struggling to join his body in the waking world. "What lady are you on about?"

"You sly dog," Jermaine said as he paced around the front room. "What lady? As if we can't smell her!"

"The floral scent," Sana said from the porch. "It's quite strong, even out here. Perhaps a hint of cinnamon sticks mixed in as well."

"What are you still doing outside, dear sister?" asked Jermaine. "Don't tell me Gaethen's naked body is something you haven't seen a thousand times in your dreams."

Gaethen looked down and started. "My goodness, I'm so sorry!" He turned and ran down the hall with one hand in front and one behind to cover up his parts. Jermaine's laughter followed him all the way to his bedroom.

Gaethen looked around the room. A pile of neatly folded clothes sat on a chair in one corner. He picked up the shirt. Two of the buttons were missing, and the garment was torn halfway down, starting at the right armpit. A mix of blood and mud streaked across the front of the shirt. He dropped it on the floor and examined the slacks. They were also caked in muck and torn at the knees. He went to the wardrobe and pulled out a fresh outfit.

"Are you finally ready to tell us what happened to you?" Jermaine asked from the kitchen. He had the fire going in the stove and had set the kettle on. Sana was scooping tea leaves into three cups.

Gaethen pulled up a chair and sat. "Last thing I remember, the sheep had gotten loose. I was surprised, what with the fence enclosing the yard and all. I kept thinking I heard some sort of growling sound while I was in here preparing supper, but it's not often that predators come out of the woods to harass my livestock. After my meal, I went out and found one of the youngest lambs, the black sheep of that litter—pieces of her, anyway, shredded and scattered around the field. Something had torn through the fence. The other sheep had disappeared entirely."

"The little gal with the white patch that looked like a crescent moon?" Sana asked.

"The very one. Born only three months ago, but I had already grown attached to her. She loved chasing me around the yard and nibbling at my pant cuffs."

"None of the neighbors seem to have been hit," Jermaine said. "It would have been the talk of the town."

"What could even do that?" Sana asked. "We grew up hearing tales about beasts in the Forest of Despair, but those were only to scare kids out of playing in the trees and getting lost."

"There was certainly *something* out there," Gaethen said. "I didn't see it, but I felt its presence, if you can believe it. Those old stories certainly did the trick, Sana; I went deeper into the forest than I had in years, but I didn't enjoy a single moment of it. I felt like I was being watched. Followed. And then came the hole."

"Ah, the old caverns of Ferathan," Jermaine said as he set one of the teacups in front of Gaethen. "We explored one of them when we were just lads, Gaeth. You remember? So we didn't fully avoid the forest back then."

"That was hardly more than a rabbit hole, though. This cavern was much, much deeper. I slipped right into it and tried to climb back up some of the roots that hung down, but then I heard movement somewhere in the darkness. I can't afford to lose the flock, so I swallowed my fear and ventured in farther. Once the panic set in, so did my wheezing. At some point, I fell into a pit and only just managed to catch on to the wall. I don't remember much else after that, but suddenly I was out in the woods in the arms of a woman."

"Of all the ways to attract a lady," Jermaine jested, "you had to go and nearly kill yourself. My sister would have been willing without all that, you know."

"Who was this heroine?" Sana asked, ignoring her brother. "Nobody in town has said anything about this incident yet!"

"I wish I knew," Gaethen said. "I have the strangest recollection about her. It almost feels like a dream. At first, she seemed to be an old hag. Ancient, really. But then, I swear I glimpsed a much younger face. Strikingly beautiful. I don't think I hit my head —I don't feel any bumps—but I can't remember clearly one way or the other."

"A witch in Ferathan," Sana said.

Gaethen spilled a bit of tea down his chin in surprise.

"You can't be serious, Sana," Jermaine said. "I've heard of the witches in the far north, and of course the practitioners down in the Aepistelle kingdoms, but nobody like that has ever bothered coming around here. The people of Ferathan are a stubbornly grounded lot. No magic, no gods, just stories to scare children. If a witch made her way here, she'd be chased out with pitchforks and torches."

"We can only hope for something so exciting to happen in this backwoods town," Gaethen said. He was jesting on the surface, but he felt deep down that perhaps Sana was right.

Perhaps a witch *had* come to Ferathan, and she had revealed herself only to him.

CHAPTER 3

Once Jermaine was convinced that Gaethen was in good health after his two-day disappearance, he and his sister left Gaethen alone and headed back to work at their family's brewery. Gaethen had put on his most collected face for them, but it had taken a great deal of effort. As soon as they left, Gaethen rushed back into his bedroom and reexamined the discarded clothing.

Am I losing my mind? he thought. *A witch came to me, of all people, and I lived to tell the tale? Not bloody likely.*

And yet, what other explanation was there? He may have been only half conscious, but Gaethen knew what he'd seen. The woman had worn two distinct faces. She had pulled him out of the pit and carried him effortlessly, as if he were a sack of feathers. The cave was at least half a mile away, but she had brought him all the way back home, undressed him, and tucked him into his bed.

The bleating of a sheep pulled Gaethen back into awareness. He tossed the clothes onto his bed and jogged out the front door. The creatures were grazing all around the yard as if they hadn't been on some adventure just two nights prior, as if one of their youngest hadn't been torn to shreds.

Gaethen approached one of the ewes and clicked his tongue at her. She didn't flinch as he stroked her fur. "Hello, there, Mama," he said to her. "Did you lose your little girl the other day? You're certainly holding up well, all things considered." The ewe rubbed her head against Gaethen's pant leg and then resumed grazing.

He made his way around the yard, examining the fence. There wasn't a single break in it, and it didn't appear that any section had been damaged and mended except portions Gaethen himself had fixed over the years. He reached the farthest corner, close to the tree line. There was no blood or other remains of the little black lamb. No sign of a struggle.

A small bleating grabbed his attention. He turned around but didn't see the source of the noise. Something rustled beyond the trees on the other side of the fence, and the bleating repeated.

"Is someone out there?" Gaethen asked. He effortlessly scaled the low fence and dropped down on the other side. Five steps into the woods, he found the source of the bleating.

Gaethen froze in his tracks.

The little black lamb met his eyes. She was in one piece, white crescent moon and all. No blood or gore. No sign of injury. They stood there looking at each other, the lamb seemingly in as much shock as the man. After a minute, Gaethen bent low and slowly moved his hand toward her.

"Thora? Well, fancy seeing you out here, tiny thing," Gaethen said. "Let's get you back home to your mama. I'm sure she's—"

The lamb lunged forward and bit Gaethen's hand. He stumbled back and fell on his bottom. The lamb turned and darted deeper into the forest.

Over the years, Gaethen had been bitten by his sheep more times than he could count. What surprised him was that the lamb had drawn blood. Gaethen glanced down to find his left pinkie and ring finger dripping crimson. In that split second in which the lamb had lunged at his hand, he thought he had seen several razor-sharp teeth in the little creature's mouth. He knew it wasn't possible. The lamb should have had only some of her lower teeth, as well as the hard pad on the roof of her mouth. The teeth he thought he had observed just then had sprouted from the top and bottom and were nothing like the sheep teeth he had seen his whole life.

Gaethen lost sight of the lamb, but he could still hear her feet shuffling through the brush. He jumped back up and ran after her.

"I'm not chasing any more of you little beasts into that cave, so don't bother going in there!" Gaethen yelled, but he knew he would do just that to save the little creature and bring her home, freakish teeth or not.

The patter of the little feet led him farther into the woods. The trees here were quite overgrown and sprouted close together. The canopy started to block out the afternoon sunlight. Gaethen felt as if he had traveled this exact route two days prior. He clicked his tongue, hoping to catch the lamb's attention, but she continued on her wayward journey.

Gaethen followed. He plowed through a massive web that had been woven between a pair of tree trunks, but he did not slow down to look for the inevitably oversize arachnid that had crafted it. A few birds flew out of the brush ahead as the wayward animal disturbed their foraging. Squirrels dodged the little creature, then doubled back when they caught sight of her pursuer. The chase continued for several minutes, until Gaethen's boot caught on a protruding root and he fell face-first to the ground, splitting his chin on a rock.

An explosion of light blinded him momentarily. Once it cleared, he peered ahead and noticed the entrance to the cave. The cries of the lamb echoed within it. She sounded distressed.

Gaethen climbed to his feet and started to jog toward the black maw, but he skidded to a halt when he heard an animalistic roar. The lamb squealed and then fell silent. The next sound was a crunch of bones. Gaethen was slowly backing away when a figure appeared at the mouth of the cave.

It was not a predator.

It was a woman. It was *her*.

CHAPTER 4

"Gaethen Devorac. You have returned to me sooner than expected."

Gaethen didn't mean to gawk, but he couldn't help himself. She was as bare as he had been when he'd gotten out of bed that morning.

"Well, it seems we've both witnessed each other in our ... *natural* state," she said. "If I want to get a coherent thought out of you, I suppose I should cover up."

She walked back into the darkness of the cave. A few moments later, she reemerged with a black wool cloak wrapped around her body. Even from twenty feet away, Gaethen could make out a particular feature of the wool.

"The moon," he said. He walked toward her.

The woman looked up at the sky and shook her head. "No moon yet, I'm afraid. It's still midday."

Gaethen neared her and reached out his hand. He ran his fingertips over the outline of the crescent moon on her cloak. "Where did you get this?" he asked.

"My, my—I didn't take you for a touchy one, Gaethen. Not on our second meeting, anyhow." She brought her right hand up and playfully patted his cheek. "I made this little garment, if you must know. There wasn't a lot to choose from in these woods, so I had to improvise. Do you like it?"

"How is it possible? My little Thora ... she was alive just minutes ago. I chased her through the forest. She even bit me when I tried to pet her ..." Gaethen held his hand up. There was no blood. No puncture wound. "I'm so confused."

"It seems like confusion has dominated your last couple of days, my dear boy. I don't blame you. These trees have power. This forest and the endless labyrinth of tunnels that run below it are known to be filled with wonders that cannot be explained. Touched by the gods, perhaps, or cursed by demons. Depends on your point of view."

"The people of Ferathan keep clear of the woods as much as possible," Gaethen said. "We get travelers passing through from time to time, coming from the Aepistelle kingdoms in the south or Emyhrsen in the north. We mostly live vicariously through their tales. I always thought the stories we heard were merely meant to keep us close to home. Are you saying there is truth in them?"

"I believe you already know the answer, after these last few days."

"And what of Thora? How is it that I was able to touch her if she was merely a spirit?"

The woman smiled. She whispered something Gaethen could not hear, though even if he had, he would not have known the words, for they were of a land and people he had never come across in his twenty-four years. She unwrapped the cloak from around her shoulders, then pulled it off. Gaethen was about to avert his eyes when he noticed she was not naked underneath, but clothed in undergarments that had not been there minutes earlier. She tossed the cloak in the air, raising her voice as she continued the chant. It had a singsong quality to it, and the melody felt familiar to him, though the words were still entirely foreign. The cloak approached the ground, but it did not fall flat; it formed the unmistakable shape of the lamb, Thora. The cloak had been much larger than the animal, but when it fell, the leftover sections became the lamb's shadow on the ground behind her.

"So you are indeed a witch," Gaethen said. He backed away from her several steps.

"I am Naliah Lunarra. I come from far to the north of here, beyond Emyhrsen and the Cascade Mountains. I mean you no harm."

"And what is it you want from me, Naliah?" Gaethen looked at the reincarnated lamb. "You snared me in your trap with that abomination. You led me here. Why?"

"Would you believe that I just wanted to see you again?" Naliah began to close the space between them. "It's true that mine is a transactional people. But this is more than that. I felt a deep connection to you the other night, deep enough to draw me to you when you were in peril. I pulled you out of what could have been a dire situation. I carried you home, cleaned your wounds, and left you to rest in safety and comfort. Perhaps instead of looking for ulterior motives, you could appreciate what I did for you and show me courtesy."

Gaethen's shoulders dropped. "You're right. I'm very sorry for the way I acted. We do not get visitors of your kind in Ferathan, only dark stories."

"It happens everywhere I go, to be honest," she said.

"Please, come to town with me. There must be a room available at one of the inns. It will be much more comfortable than this cave, if that's where you've been sleeping. If you do not have the money for such a stay, I can set up a bed for you at my farm in one of the unused laborer cottages."

Naliah smiled. She turned to what had once been Gaethen's precious little black lamb and whistled. The lamb—*it*—returned to her. Naliah reached down and pulled at the wool, which immediately collapsed into a lifeless, flaccid piece of clothing again. She wrapped it around her shoulders and took Gaethen's hand.

"Thank you, Gaethen. You won't regret this."

But deep inside, Gaethen knew that he just might.

CHAPTER 5

The strange occurrences on the other farms began within a day. Cows were found mutilated or outright missing from the Soltani family's pasture the morning after Gaethen brought the mysterious visitor into Ferathan. It didn't cross his mind that his guest could have been responsible; she was with him the whole day, and she retired to the cottage nearest his dwelling once night fell. It also helped that much about their first two meetings had mysteriously escaped his memory.

A day after that, four women returned from their usual hunting trip in the eastern foothills known as the Fingers. They were in good health, but the problem was that they had set out as a team of twelve. The other eight—all men—had been attacked and consumed by giants known as the Ogressi. It had been years since the Ogressi had been spotted so near Ferathan, and when the massive beasts had attacked back then, they had picked off one or two men at most. Eight was a full-blown slaughter.

That night, wolves howled all around the town. It was as if they were circling the perimeter of Ferathan, daring the residents to come out and face them. The following morning, the Abels found every last fruit in their entire grove of apple trees shriveled up and covered in flies. On the day after that, the Galens ran into town, screaming that the fresh eggs laid by their hens were full not of yolk and whites but of pure crimson blood. Everyone laughed at them—Hector Galen was known to be jealous anytime the spotlight was on someone else—until Constable Buckland followed them home and witnessed the bloody eggs for himself. Hector claimed he had looked out his bedroom window the night before and spotted a mysterious but beautiful woman in the darkness, who must have cursed his hens. The town just laughed at him once again, seemingly forgetting the strangeness that had just been proven minutes earlier.

Gaethen wasn't alone in his oblivion. He took Naliah Lunarra all around town, trying out various restaurants, perusing the latest books imported from the south of Aepistelle, and socializing with people. Everywhere they went, Naliah seemed to charm those around her. Gaethen watched with pride—and perhaps something a bit more romantic—as his guest became the star of the town. The residents were spellbound by her stories about the places she'd visited, the exotic animals she'd come across, and the people she'd met. She spoke of dining with the young King Harold of Emyhrsen shortly before arriving in Ferathan, which sparked the attention and jealousy of many of the ladies; the young royal was quite the heartthrob and an unlikely bachelor.

Perhaps her most ardent admirers were the children of Ferathan, and she was as equally smitten with them. She taught them games, such as drawing rows of squares on the sidewalk and hopping in and out of them on one foot. She ran around the grassy field in the central park, chasing them. It was as if she had lost her younger years to unknown hardships and was now finally living out her youthful whimsies. Gaethen even joined in on some of the games, kicking a ball around the field, letting the children win, and laughing without a care in the world. In those moments, he caught a look on Naliah's face when her gaze met his, as if she was seeing an opportunity in him. As if there was something she wanted deep down, something he wanted just as much for the first time in years—a family.

There was one person who was not enamored with the newcomer. Jermaine Fielder knew what most of the folks in Ferathan did not: that the mysterious woman had been there during Gaethen's near-death experience a few nights prior and was more than likely the cause of the whole fiasco.

"It's clear that all the recent afflictions of this town are being caused by this *Naliah Lunarra*," Jermaine ranted to his sister in their backyard. Sana was enjoying the late-morning sun while picking floral hops. The cone-shaped flowers would be used in the ales made at the brewery they operated with their parents. Fielders' Fancies was a favorite not only among the people of Ferathan but throughout Emyhrsen to the north, especially that kingdom's ruler and his court. "The way Gaethen is blinded by her makes me think he's already under some kind of spell."

"Yes, it's called love," Sana said as she dropped a handful of hops into her basket. "He's always been quite oblivious to it. I couldn't draw the man's attention no matter how hard I tried to flirt with him, but Naliah seems to be just what he didn't know he wanted all this time."

"I honestly wasn't even sure he was interested in women! He's been my closest friend for our entire lives, yet he's never joined me in pursuing the ladies in town. Don't worry, sister—I've tried to sell him on you as well. I would love to call him my brother as well as my best pal. It's not too late, though. We'll get him to see her for what she is."

"You don't really believe she's a witch, do you?" Sana asked.

"And why wouldn't I? With all that's happened in this town since she arrived, how could there be any other explanation?"

"I quite like her, dear brother. Her charisma is very contagious. Everyone in town seems happier with her around, even in the midst of the tragedies that have been occurring. Can you really tell me that you wouldn't feel the same as Gaethen if she had carried *you* to your bed and undressed you?"

"Well, my brain says I'd still not trust her. I suppose my loins might say otherwise, but I thought Gaethen of all people would be driven by what's upstairs and not what's downstairs."

"He's a man, same as you. Now, pick up those baskets, and let's get back to the brewery. Dad is loading up the wagon while we dawdle here."

It wasn't a long walk. They went out the back gate and down the alley behind their house, which led them to the town's main street. One block up was the bustling restaurant that kept the family quite busy. It was a profitable operation, and they were able to employ line cooks and servers to take care of the customers up front while the family focused on the business aspects and the brewery.

"About bloody time," their father said as they walked through the back door of the establishment.

"I thought I'd have to make these deliveries myself. Maybe then I'd get to have a toast with that young king of the north. I'm sure he has quite a flock of beautiful women fawning over him in his audience chamber. Or his bedchamber."

"Jonathan!" Jermaine's mother scoffed. "Stop corrupting my boy. I'm sure that King Harold is an honorable young man. He is royalty, after all."

"We've all heard the stories, Mum," Sana said. "Dad is probably not too far off, but Jermaine is just the delivery boy. He only ever sees the back door of the castle."

Jermaine climbed up on the cart, took the reins, and started forward. "I choose to be unobtrusive, sure, but if I wanted to meet with King Harold, I think that could be arranged. We brew his favorite beverage, after all."

Sana walked alongside the cart as it crept down the alley. "Take care, Jer. Don't let the thieves seize our wares on the road!"

Jermaine halted the horses and turned to his sister with a concerned expression. "Listen, Sana—I need you to keep an eye on Gaethen. I hate to leave him at such a strange time. I'm going to speak with the staff at the castle about Naliah Lunarra. She claims she spent time at King Harold's court, so someone there must know something about her. I'll see you in a few days."

"Be careful. If she is as evil as you fear, she may have some dark allies there who will warn her about you poking around."

"If she's as evil as I fear, there won't be any town left to come home to." With that, Jermaine began his journey northwest around Lake Ferathan, where he would catch a ferry at Frogstown to King Harold's Keep on the opposite side of the Amassa River.

Sana had only just begun her latest chore—cleaning out barrels from the previous brews to prepare them for the next batch—when her mother interrupted.

"Honey, you have a visitor out in the dining hall." Mrs. Fielder winked at her daughter. "May want to freshen up before you go see him, though."

Sana set her sponge aside and dried off her hands on a nearby rag. "Don't worry, Mum. I'm not impressing any men around here. I think I need to seek out a proper northern man."

"Well, he didn't ask for your brother, did he? Go on. Don't keep him waiting."

Sana cut through the kitchen, nimbly weaving between the cooks charring meats and blackening vegetables over open flames. She went through the doorway into the restaurant's dining hall, catching several disappointed glances when hungry patrons realized it wasn't their meals being delivered.

Standing near the front entrance was her brother's best friend.

"Why, Gaethen, what brings you here? I didn't expect to see you without your new lady friend! At least you're fully clothed this time." Sana looked around. There wasn't an open table, so she led him outside. "Let's walk, and you can tell me what's on your mind. I need some fresh air anyway."

Gaethen didn't speak as they began their walk down Ferathan's main avenue, so Sana turned to him. He was wearing a grin that stretched his cheeks and revealed the dimples that had always made her blush.

"Well, Gaethen Devorac, if I didn't know any better, I'd say you were in love."

"That's just it, Sana. I don't know if it's love or confusion or something else. I've never felt this way about anyone, so I can't even explain what it's like."

"And why didn't you talk to my brother about this? He's your closest pal."

"Yes, and he's been with many women before. But that's just it. He's been with lots of women and has never truly loved any of them. What does he know about love?"

"He knows about as little as you do, apparently," Sana said.

Gaethen halted and reached for her arm, gently stopping her and turning her to face him. "So you think it's not love, then? I trust your judgement. What would you call it?"

"Infatuation, perhaps?" Sana shrugged and thought carefully about what to say next, not wanting to burst whatever bubble he was floating in. "You've only known her mere days. Outsiders have an allure that attracts all of us in a small town like this. But I don't blame you for feeling this way, especially considering how much special attention she's given you and how she saved you from whatever happened a few nights ago. It's only natural that you formed some kind of bond with her."

Gaethen had a distant but blissful look in his eyes, as if he was in the midst of a wonderful dream from which he did not want to wake. His voice was soft when he spoke again. "Yes, perhaps you're right. I don't know. I think it's more than that."

"Well, maybe it's—"

"Yes, more than that," he interrupted, as if he didn't hear her anymore. "Tonight I am going to ask her to marry me."

CHAPTER 6

On the outskirts of town, there was a scuffling in the brush at the edge of the road. Jermaine looked down from the driver's box, where he had been daydreaming as he rode the same route he'd taken dozens of times before. No creature appeared, so Jermaine shook it off and looked ahead. The road was deserted, as it usually was.

Another three hours passed without event. Jermaine was enjoying the view of Lake Ferathan on his right when something slammed hard against the cart from the west side of the road. The cart was piled high with full barrels and was quite heavy, but whatever hit it had enough force to tilt it up several inches. Jermaine didn't even have time to look before he lost his balance and fell off on the lake side.

The road sat on the edge of a bluff alongside the water with only a small rocky bank at the bottom of the decline. Jermaine failed to grab the front wheel of the wagon, his only chance at breaking the fall. He tumbled, crunching over every rock that jutted out of the ground on the way down. One of them gashed open his right cheek. He tried to grab hold of an outcropping of weeds to slow his descent, but his left pinkie caught in a knot of stems and was bent backward. He plummeted into the lake with a large splash.

The water wasn't as shallow as he had expected. He sank down and down before finally touching the bottom fifteen feet below. He was seeing stars from slamming his head countless times on the descent, and his cheek stung. In his stupor, he didn't even fight to reach the surface; he merely looked up toward it.

On the bank, illuminated by a ray of sunshine, was a woman. Because of the water and his own hazy vision, he couldn't quite make out her features, but he didn't need to. He knew exactly who it was.

A man ran directly through her as if she was not solid. He didn't even appear to have noticed her as he dove into the lake fully clothed. He made it down to Jermaine, grabbed him by the arms, and pulled him up to the surface.

When Jermaine came to several minutes later, he was back up the hill, lying in the middle of the road.

"I wanted you in the direct sunlight so you'd dry off quicker. That lake is mighty cold, my friend."

Jermaine's vision came back to him, and he took in the sight of the man standing over him. The rescuer was fully bald and sported a soggy mustache that drooped at the sides of his mouth. Jermaine didn't have to ask who the man was.

"What in blazes is a priest of Solendaron doing up here?" Jermaine asked. He looked around and found the man's clothes, an especially fine suit, draped over the wheels of Jermaine's cart.

"Ah, so you can tell even with my mustache in this flaccid state? I suppose we do stand out in any scenario, as we are meant to." The man reached down and helped Jermaine sit up. "My name is Arun of Esteron—a priest of Solendaron, as you noted. I'm on my way down south from Emyhrsen, heading back home. I was squatting in the trees on the other side of the road when I heard your splash."

"I'm lucky you were there, then, Arun of Esteron."

"Luck has no part in it. Our meeting was the will of the lord Solendaron."

Jermaine wanted to laugh, but he thought twice and decided not to offend the man who had just saved him from an early death. Suddenly, a vision of Naliah Lunarra at the edge of the lake flashed into his mind.

"The woman! Did you see her? It looked as if you ran right through her when you jumped in to rescue me."

"Woman? There was no woman, friend. I thought you must have sampled a little too much of your stock and taken a drunken tumble, though I soon learned that wasn't true. There was no taste of ale in your mouth when I breathed life back into you."

"And what of the beast? Did you see or hear whatever creature stampeded through the woods at a velocity that nearly tipped the entire cart?"

"What did this beast look like?"

Jermaine shook his head. "I didn't see it, nor did I hear it approaching. But it had to have been there."

Arun stared into his eyes with a depth and intensity that forced Jermaine to turn away. The logical part of his mind trusted the priest, but some other part made him wonder if the man was indeed real or merely a specter, like whatever he'd seen standing at the edge of the lake. *No, that's foolish*, he thought. *A spirit would not have been able to lift my body out of the water and drag me up the hill.* He shook off the idea.

"Then I imagined the whole thing, I suppose. Or ..."

"Or something evil is at play here," Arun said. "I see no deceit in your eyes. Fear and confusion, but no malice. It seems we must be cautious out here."

"You may find just as much danger in Ferathan as you pass through," Jermaine warned. "There have been many strange occurrences in town these last few days. Be cautious."

"Would you like me to check on anyone while I'm there? I plan to stay the night at an inn and restock my travel supplies before venturing through the long stretch of forest."

"Since you're offering, I must ask that you keep an eye out for my dearest friend, Gaethen Devorac. I believe he's closest to the one who has afflicted the town. She seems to have charmed him in some way."

"Women have a way of doing that, just as men have ways of leading women astray. But, as you've requested, I will look in on this friend of yours. I will let him know you are thinking of him during your journey."

Arun pulled his clothes from the wagon wheels and began to dress again. Jermaine turned away and stared into the woods, where the unseen beast must have come from. There were no broken branches, nothing to indicate that anything had come charging out to attack him. He turned back to Arun, who was now dressed and dabbing his fingers into a small jar of beeswax to shape his mustache.

"Please also let Gaethen know that I'll be gone longer than expected," Jermaine said. "I have to figure out a few things while I'm in Emyhrsen. He'll pass the message on to my family so they don't worry about me."

And with that, they said their goodbyes and parted ways.

CHAPTER 7

Harold's ascent to the throne of Emyhrsen had come unexpectedly early, but it had been completely free of drama or intrigue. His father had been an only child, as was he. There had been no close relatives to try and hold regency due to his age, nor anyone to dispute Harold's right to the throne. Even had someone attempted, they would not have gotten far. Harold and his father were deeply beloved in Emyhrsen, and the people had celebrated his crown as vigorously as they had mourned his father's passing.

Like his father, Harold was a man of the people and was not above spending time among them. He could be found dining at restaurants in all the villages he visited. He knew many of his people by name. He only stopped short of appearing as entertainment at children's birthday parties because there was not enough time in the day.

And, at seventeen years old, he was also prone to drinking and merrymaking with his close friends, whom he kept in his court by giving them advisory titles. He kept the elder generation of advisors from his father's rule around as well, but he knew that the kingdom would have to continue to adapt in order to be progressive in their ever-changing world, and he thought his friends could help him attain that goal. Edward Smythe was one such friend.

"I do apologize, but His Majesty will not be able to see you," Edward said. "He is unwell at the moment. He will be absolutely overjoyed to hear that these casks have arrived, though. Perhaps that will give him the pick-me-up he needs. Your family makes his favorite ales."

"I'm very sorry to hear that the king is ill," Jermaine said. He gestured around the castle's court-yard. "I hope there is nothing serious going around. Everyone looks a little more glum than usual. It's unnatural in this place."

"Yes, well, it's nothing contagious, so no need to worry. We will all be back at the old song and dance by week's end, I'm sure." But Edward's face betrayed whatever optimism he tried to exude. It was unnat-ural, and Jermaine didn't like it.

"Perhaps you can help me, then, Edward. It's about a woman."

Edward stumbled back, and the color faded from his cheeks as if Jermaine had told him his mother had died. "A woman? I ... I don't know that the king and I can help you with your relationship problems. Perhaps you had better seek counsel elsewhere."

Jermaine wasn't sure if Edward was just bashful on the topic of the opposite sex, seeing as he was barely past puberty, or if there was something else going on. Edward turned and started to walk away when Jermaine called out to him. "Her name is Naliah Lunarra," he said. Edward stopped in his tracks but did not turn around. "I believe she's a witch."

"And why do you think it is necessary to trouble the king or me about this supposed witch?"

"I think you know why. I think she's been here, and I think you know exactly who—and what —she is."

Edward turned and stared intently at him.

"If King Harold got rid of her," Jermaine continued, "I'd like to know how he did it without her burning down this castle."

Edward walked back to Jermaine and lowered his voice. "She left the castle intact, sure, but some of its inhabitants did not get out unscathed." He looked around. Some of the castle's staff was still unloading the casks of ale from Jermaine's cart. "I'll have the stable master put up your horses. Follow me, and I'll make sure a room is prepared for you. I'll give you one night here. We'll see if the king is willing to speak to you by this time tomorrow. If not, it's back on the ferry for you."

The staff inside the castle looked more dour than Jermaine had ever seen them. As Edward led him through the service halls to a room in the midst of the servants' quarters, he noted that most of the staff avoided eye contact, and those whose gaze he did meet looked at him distrustfully.

This did not feel like the warm and welcoming place he visited twice each year. He didn't like it at all.

A KNOCK WOKE JERMAINE EARLY THE NEXT morning. As he wiped the sleep from his eyes, the door opened. A young maid of ten or eleven opened the door and peered in at the visitor.

"King Harold is ready for you, sir," she said. "I'll be outside the door when you're ready, but don't keep His Majesty waiting long."

Once she shut the door, Jermaine sat up, threw back his blankets, and dressed hastily. He didn't have the time—or the outfit—to make himself presentable, so he didn't bother doing more than running his fingers through his hair, hoping to tame his bedhead.

The girl was waiting for him in the hall. "I'm Adelina, but people call me Addy. Come this way." She led him through the narrow walkways, zigzagging between busy servants, sacks of laundry, and suspicious stares.

"Thanks for coming to get me, Addy. Aren't you a bit young to work in the castle?"

She glanced back but kept up her speed. "Nonsense! The king himself was hardly out of diapers when I was born, and he's leading the bloody country. Besides, my mum is a seamstress here, as is her mum, as I'll probably be too. My pa is part of the castle guard. I have nowhere else to go." She led him down a stairwell. "Now, he's in quite a mood again today. It's been a strange couple of weeks here already, so try not to make it worse."

They approached a set of doors flanked by two guards on each side. Jermaine surmised by the proud nod one of them gave to Addy that the man was her father. The doors opened onto a long audience chamber. Addy walked in ahead of Jermaine, leading him over an elaborately stitched red carpet. She bowed in front of the dais on which stood a throne. Jermaine caught up and did the same.

"Mister Jermaine Fielder of Ferathan, Your Majesty," the girl announced. She turned and walked to the back of the room, leaving him alone in front of the king.

"Ah, Fielder, how I could have used your ales over the past weeks to drown my sorrows," the king said. He was slouched in a manner that would have brought shame to the tutors of his youth. "The brewers of Emyhrsen could certainly learn a thing or two from your family. Perhaps I should send them down to your humble town to take a few notes from your father."

"It's my honor to deliver our wares to you, Your Majesty," Jermaine said.

Harold signaled to a servant standing off to one side. The man stepped behind a curtain and returned a moment later with a mug of ale, to Jermaine's surprise.

"We've already tapped one of the barrels. I hope you don't mind me drinking in front of you. It makes quite a breakfast." Harold took a long gulp of the dark brew. "And what is it you wanted to speak to me about?"

"It's about a visitor we've had in Ferathan. A woman who calls herself Naliah Lunarra."

The king choked on his beer. The servant rushed over and took the glass from him as he recovered. "Ms. Lunarra, you say? Is she causing trouble for you down in Ferathan? We had a beast of a time with her here."

"Well, we've had some rather odd occurrences around town that coincided with her arrival. I suspect that she's ..." Jermaine looked around. He was embarrassed to say it. His voice shrank considerably. "A witch."

The young monarch stared at him in silence for a moment. Then a smile broke out on his face, followed by laughter. "Oh, you just 'suspect it,' do you?" More laughter mocked Jermaine. "Well, friend, there's no suspicion needed. She certainly is a witch, and she's a bloody dangerous one. Be careful, Fielder. Be very careful indeed."

"What did she do to you here, Your Majesty?"

Harold rose from his throne and stepped off the dais. He waved for Jermaine to follow, and the visitor obliged. They walked through a doorway behind a curtain and into a smaller room featuring a dining table full of food. "Sit," the king ordered, and Jermaine obeyed. In a flash, three servants filled their plates and then exited the room, leaving Jermaine alone with the king.

"I haven't been sleeping well lately. Look at this spread: breakfast, lunch, and supper, rolled into one. The servants don't even know what to feed me anymore, as I sleep in the afternoon and break my fast in the middle of the night."

Harold stuffed his mouth with eggs and a meat pie. Jermaine couldn't resist the mash-up of meals; he was famished from the journey, and Edward hadn't sent any food to his room the previous evening. He ate voraciously and waited for the king to supply information at his own speed. In the meantime, Jermaine offered small talk about the brewing process and his sister's experiments with different hops and grains.

"I should like to meet your sister one of these days, Fielder. Perhaps she can travel here with you on the next delivery run."

"She would certainly love that, Your Majesty. She's only been up to Emyhrsen a couple of times for the big Fair of the North when we were children. We were probably just around your age the last time, eight or so years ago."

Harold's fork and knife clattered as he dropped them on his plate. "My age, yes." He looked at Jermaine. "My age is something to be spoken of by all who regard me, it seems."

"I'm sorry, Your Majesty. I didn't mean anything by the comment."

"Oh, no, I know you did not mean to offend. You're a good man, Fielder. I like you a lot. It's just that there are some who would try to take advantage of me due to my lack of years in this world."

Jermaine pressed his luck. "And is Naliah Lunarra one of those you speak of?"

"Precisely so." King Harold looked resignedly at

Jermaine as if he knew there was no reason to hold back. "She came to us as a girl my very age. She's so strikingly beautiful, and just different enough from the other girls I know to make it clear she is not from around here. She came to my court only about two moons ago. It was very quick, really; that was all she needed to get us in her grasp. She charmed me. I invited her to sit right where you are now, and she took all her meals with me. She whispered in my ear when I had callers in the audience chamber, gave me advice on matters of state. I took her out and showed her the land, and we greeted my people together."

There was a long pause as Harold thought back. "One evening, as my courtiers and I were staying at an inn on the western end of my kingdom, I heard a noise outside. It was a full moon that night, so when I looked out the window of my second-floor suite, I saw her clearly on a low hilltop nearby. I put my clothes on and tiptoed out to her so as not to wake my guards. As I neared the hill, she turned to me. Her hair blew in the breeze, and that's when I saw something that didn't look right. It was not that stark red, but silver. I took a few steps closer, but she quickly turned and ran down the other side. But before she was over the crest, I got a good look at her. She wasn't a girl my age at all, but an old crone. Wrinkled skin. Gnarled hands."

"It's ... she ..." Jermaine couldn't get the words out. For once in his life, he didn't know what to say.

"It's impossible, it's insane, I know. But it happened. I ran up to the top of the hill, and when I looked down, she was on her way back up from the other side. She looked normal, the same gorgeous young woman I'd known for nearly a month. She grabbed my hand, and I remember it felt shockingly cold for a split second. She kissed me on the cheek, and we walked silently back to the inn and parted ways for the night.

"The next morning, the innkeeper complained that his dogs had gone missing. I sent a couple of my guards out to help find the mutts, and they returned shortly after with a report that the dogs had been located on the far side of the hill, the side Naliah had gone to in the night. They were dead, savagely mutilated."

Jermaine dropped his fork, which snapped him out of his stupor. "I'm sorry. I can't believe what I'm hearing, yet it's not far off from what happened to a friend of mine back home. Dead animals, shifting appearances. And she charmed him as well. He's completely blind to what she really is."

"Your friend may be in danger. I was her target here, and perhaps your friend is the one she has latched on to in Ferathan."

"You made it out alive, though, Your Majesty. What happened after that occurrence?"

"She acted quite normal after that. I didn't see her do anything too unusual, but I also grew quite distant from her. She knew what I had witnessed, and she didn't try to convince me that it was a trick of the light or anything. A couple of weeks later, she told me that she had to move on. In the middle of the night, she was gone. I had assumed she went back up north rather than down to Ferathan. I wasn't sad that she left, but since she's been gone, it's as if the lifeblood of this entire castle has been drained. Sucked out by a leech, if you will. Everyone feels lethargic and just ... off."

"Good for you for recognizing it. You are a wise man in the body of a boy." Jermaine drained his mug as he pondered the situation. As much as he wanted to head back home to check on Gaethen, he felt that there was still much to learn. "You said she came from the north. Where exactly in the north?"

"I'm not certain. She was brought to the castle by a textile merchant we do business with. Melchin, his name is. He may be able to tell you more. We haven't seen him since then."

"And where can I find this Melchin?" Jermaine asked.

"He comes down from Elm Springs, three days'

ride north of here. If you stay on the main road, you won't miss it."

Jermaine stood up. "If you don't mind, then, I'll take my leave now. I must learn more about this woman before I return home."

"I hope there is a home to return to, Fielder. Be careful. Whatever she is, there is a dark power within her. Why she left us mostly unscathed, I'm not certain, but it seems as if we only narrowly missed some kind of disaster."

Jermaine said his farewells, then let Addy lead him out to the stable master. The king had already sent the order for the safekeeping of Jermaine's cart and one of his horses. Jermaine saddled up the other horse and sped away from the castle along the road to the north.

CHAPTER 8

Gaethen had always imagined that his wedding ceremony would include his best friend standing beside him to cheer him on and give him the boost of confidence that Jermaine always had a way of providing. But Naliah had not gotten to know Jermaine, and she did not have any close friends of her own to balance things out, even had Jermaine actually been in town.

There were no surviving members of the Devorac bloodline to share in the celebration of such a momentous occasion, but all the Fielders had always been like family to Gaethen. So, while Jermaine had not yet returned from his trip to the north, Gaethen seemed content with the presence of Sana and her parents at the ceremony.

They were set up on the grounds of Ferathan

Manor, a rather castle-like structure on the northeast edge of the town. The residence housed Mayor Coran Wylder and her extended family, though the occupants of the house were as temporary as their time in office. For Coran, though, it worked out nicely. She was in her sixth term—and twenty-fifth year—in office with no sign of change on the horizon, as long as the unfortunate happenings around town calmed down before the next election cycle.

The grounds of the estate were ornately decorated with grotesque statues of beasts both real and imaginary, including animal-human hybrids. Naliah had already learned that the people of Ferathan didn't consider themselves a superstitious lot; they practiced no official religion, nor were there any places of worship in town. Yet they all seemed afraid of what would happen if the decrepit statues were removed from the estate, despite even the oldest of them not knowing when they had been created or for what purpose. Everyone just looked down at their feet anytime they entered the grounds.

For Naliah, though, the statues were an attraction. The wedding could have taken place in the usual spot for such occasions, but the central park was dull, in her opinion, when the children weren't there, running around and filling the air with laughter. Gaethen wasn't one to argue with the woman who held him in the chains of love, so he had gone directly to Mayor Coran Wylder and asked if she'd allow them the use of the manor grounds for the wedding. He had told her it was Naliah's request, and, like everyone in town, she didn't see any benefit to refusing Naliah her desires. They had set up for the ceremony directly on the main path leading up to the mansion, in between a statue of an elephant with three snakelike trunks that ended in mouths of sharp fangs and that of an enormous lion with the oversize head of a raven brutally pecking out a man's eyes.

The location suited Naliah well.

"Gaethen Devorac, last of your bloodline," the mayor said as she officiated the union, "with this ceremony, you lock your inner and outer self to this woman. Your love, your anger, your fears, your sorrow, your laughter, and your cries will all be one with hers. Your land and titles, your belongings, your debts and riches will all be hers to share. This is a covenant that binds you to her, and you agree to it before the eyes of Ferathan. All witnesses present today are bound by duty to hold you accountable to this covenant. Do you agree to take Naliah Lunarra as your wife and partner, granting her all that has been listed, and honor all that is promised to her?"

"I do," Gaethen said. He held Naliah's hands in his own. Their eyes were locked together intimately, as if they were alone.

Mayor Wylder asked the same of Naliah. She agreed as well, and the ceremony was complete.

Nearly every man and woman in town had shown up for the ceremony. As Gaethen and Naliah sealed their union with a kiss, the people cheered. Little did they realize that their own fate was being sealed with that kiss. The beloved stranger was now not just a wanderer. She belonged to Ferathan.

And Ferathan belonged to her.

THE PROCESSION MADE ITS WAY DOWN THE SLIGHT hill from the manor into the town—everyone except the children, who were served dinner and dessert in the great halls of Ferathan Manor. They passed the houses that lined the outer blocks; those few who hadn't attended the ceremony joined in to the march with their fellow citizens. Even without drink in them, they were a merry group, singing and laughing together. Their route went through the grassy park at the center of town and crossed the street to Fielders' Fancies, where dozens of extra tables were set up on the patio and all along the sidewalk and street in front of the brewery. Everyone found a chair, a mug, a snack. While Sana and her family provided the libations, the rest of the town had brought their favorite dishes to pass around and share.

Letty Sorvid tapped on a glass with her spoon. The sound magnified as the rest of the crowd did the same. Naliah turned to her new husband, unsure what the ruckus was for.

"It's a kiss they want," Gaethen said. "I suppose they didn't get enough back at the ceremony." He leaned slowly toward Naliah, and she grabbed him by the shirt collar and pulled him in. She gave him a kiss she was certain was the most passionate one he had ever received. The crowd went wild.

"I think I could get used to this, my love," Naliah said when she finally separated her lips from his. "It's like we're royalty."

"You would make the most beautiful queen. I'm only lucky you didn't stay long enough in Emyhrsen for the young king to have his way with you."

It was true that had she stayed in Emyhrsen any longer, she probably would have been involved in an entirely different wedding. Harold was fun. Powerful. Younger even than Gaethen. But she knew that if she had married him, it would have been for the wrong reasons. That realization hadn't come to her until she had met Gaethen on that fateful night in the cave.

"Oh, he's just a boy. No match for a man like you, Gaethen." She leaned in and kissed him again, not bothering to wait for another round of chiming glasses. She looked around the crowd as the guests turned toward the food on their tables. "This is so wonderful, Gaethen. I do wish the children were here, though. They're such a fun bunch."

"I do too, but it's tradition in Ferathan to separate the children from the adults at wedding receptions. I don't know why, but I suspect it's because when Ferathani folk celebrate, they drink a *lot*, and they don't want their children to witness them making fools of themselves." Naliah followed his gaze as Gaethen turned to face the elder Mrs. Fielder, who was bringing a spread of delicious appetizers to the bride and groom.

The meal was as glorious as it was varied: fresh fruits and vegetables from the farms that hadn't been affected by the mysterious happenings of late; juicy meats from the livestock that had survived the freak attacks, grilled to perfection; the largest catches brought in from Lake Ferathan by the fishermen. The local bakers had brought their finest cakes and pies. Every face was either being stuffed with delicious morsels or kissed by loved ones. Several of the town's musicians brought out their instruments and formed makeshift bands, and people sang along to recognizable tunes.

It was as if nobody remembered the circumstances that had been plaguing the town. Naliah wouldn't have had it any other way. All she had gone through before she'd arrived in Ferathan, all she had done in her short time in the town so far, was but a distant, forgotten memory.

And then the visitor showed up.

Just as Naliah had captivated the townspeople upon her arrival, the citizens of Ferathan let their songs fade, and a hush fell over them at the sight of the newcomer. He was an odd-looking fellow. The top of his head was hairless, but he more than made up for it with his upper lip, where an absurdly large, twisting mustache extended to both sides. His clothing was not that of the average traveler; he was dressed in a dapper suit, dirtied from the road but no less elegant for it. Many of the people recognized him immediately as a clergyman of the Solendaron faith, though the religion had no followers in their part of the continent. What they did not understand was the fear they felt when they saw him.

"Men and women of this fine town, I am Arun of Esteron. As you likely know, I am a priest of Solendaron. I have come to warn you about a threat to your peaceful existence, as far out from society as this place is. You see, while you partake in merriment, eating and drinking, laughing and singing, you are digging your own graves. You are giving up your freedoms. You are honoring someone—nay, some*thing*—completely evil."

Hushed murmurs spread through the crowd. The visitor turned his eyes toward one particular table, and everyone followed his gaze. He was looking at the new bride.

"Yes, see her for what she is. Naliah Lunarra may have come to this place with stories of adventure, tales of love, descriptions of exotic locations she has visited. But has she told you what she did in those places? How she left each one of them?"

The crowd grew louder in their confusion.

"You see, I have followed her trail of blood. I have seen firsthand the destruction she has left in her wake. She is not the beautiful young woman your eyes deceive you into seeing. Oh no, she is not at all young.

"She is one of the Azhelda, a society of sorceresses from a thousand miles north of here who live for centuries. They feed off the lifeblood of the lovers they take, but that is not enough to sustain them. So they take hold of villages as well. They find ways to gain power over the people, and they feed off that. When they've exhausted the resources of one location, they discard the broken citizens and move on."

Gaethen turned to Naliah. For the first time, it looked as if he were seeing her clearly. The haze of enchantment that had clouded his mind since the night in the cave had dispersed.

"Naliah? What is this man talking about? It's—" A rattling sound emanated from Gaethen's chest.

"Don't listen to him, Gaethen. He's clearly a madman."

"That night when you rescued me, was that a setup? Was that your way of ensnaring us?" Gaethen looked out at the townspeople who had gathered to celebrate their matrimony, then turned back to her. His wheezing grew stronger, and he hunched forward, but it wasn't enough to stop him from questioning his new bride. "Did you use me so you could destroy all of them? What have you done? What have you made *me* do?"

"No," Naliah said. She reached her hands out and placed them on Gaethen's cheeks. She felt his tears and knew that her own were flooding down her face. "Lover, no! It's not like that at all. I fell for you the moment I saw you. I knew in my heart that we could have all I have ever longed for."

"Do not fall for her evil charms, dear people of Ferathan," Arun said from across the crowd.

The people turned back toward the newlyweds and cried out in shock. The groom was turning blue, struggling to breathe. He hunched down, his head in his bride's lap.

"Gaethen, what's happening?" Naliah asked. She looked around as if desperate for help.

"She could help him," the priest said, "but she chooses not to. She wouldn't want to reveal her true powers in front of everyone."

Sana Fielder ran over and laid Gaethen down on the ground between the chairs. She started to pump on his chest as Naliah looked on and cried. For all her powers, Naliah had never felt as helpless as she did seeing her new husband on the brink of death. She froze in fear and could only watch as Gaethen continued to gasp for air despite Sana's best efforts.

Sana looked up at Naliah. "If you're really what that man says you are, why won't you help? Prove you love him and *do* something!"

Naliah looked at the townspeople through her tears. There was a mix of hatred, fear, and confusion on their faces. She hadn't lost all of them—not yet, anyway. There had to be a way to maintain her hold on them. She closed her eyes and whispered something in a tongue none of them recognized. When she completed her incantation, she bent down and put her mouth on Gaethen's. She breathed into him while Sana continued to pump on his chest.

And then the screams started.

Several large and grotesque creatures made their way across the manicured lawn of the central park across from the brewery. Their growls overpowered the people of Ferathan's gasps of disbelief. Mayor Coran Wylder's husband, Bernal, was closest to the creatures, and in bravery or stupidity, he walked toward them and recognized them for what they were.

"The statues!" he yelled. "They've come to life! They've come from the manor!"

Before he could make any additional observations, the mutant elephant stampeded toward him. He turned as if to run from it, but two of its serpentine trunks reached for him, stopping him in his tracks. The third trunk stretched open its mouth, bearing its razor-sharp teeth, and consumed the man's head.

While the rest of the town was distracted by the gruesome attack, Naliah stood over Gaethen's struggling body and spoke in her foreign tongue again. Sana was the only witness as Naliah's body began to change. Her hair grayed. Her skin sagged. Her true form was revealed in that moment, as deeply as she despised it. She bent down and breathed life back into Gaethen. When she raised her head again, she appeared just as Sana and the rest of the town had always known her: a gorgeous young woman.

Gaethen sat up. His breath met no resistance. It was as if nothing had ever impeded his airflow.

"Naliah, what ...?"

"Hush, my dear," Naliah said. She was kneeling in front of him, just enough to block his view of the chaos in the street. She pulled his face to her chest and wrapped her arms around him. Sana stood by in horror. The screams and cries for help continued, but

Naliah continued to hold her lover for another minute.

Sana finally found her voice. "Naliah, it's time to stop this."

Naliah looked at her in silence, then nodded. She closed her eyes and whispered something neither Gaethen nor Sana could understand. When Sana turned back toward the carnage, the creatures were disappearing one by one. The last one she saw was a tiger with massive wings. It was thirty feet in the air with Lester Greene dangling from its jaws by the arm. When it disappeared into nothingness, Lester fell to the gravel in a deathly plummet.

With the creatures gone, silence fell over the crowd. Half the people turned and faced the priest while the other half looked toward the witch.

In unison, Naliah and Arun pointed at each other and yelled, "You did this!"

The town didn't seem to care who to blame just yet. They were far removed from any other society; neither suspected party was going anywhere. Everyone picked up their belongings, found their loved ones, and walked back to their homes.

Sana looked on in confusion as Lester Greene stood, clearly in perfect health, and Bernal Wylder walked away with his head fully intact.

She turned back to the bride and groom, but they were already half a block away, hand in hand.

Only Arun remained.

"You have now witnessed what that woman is capable of," Arun said. "She let you see her true form, but she won't let you live to tell. She'll be back for you when you least expect it. Be careful, young lady. Be very careful indeed."

The priest turned and walked back to his camp in the forest at the edge of town.

CHAPTER 9

"Way I see it, the girl and the young king had a wild fling and a harsh breakup. Heartbroken, he is. Surprised he let her go. Real beauty. Not every day you see a woman like that on the side of the road, asking for a ride. You know, it's always been my dream to find me a wife that way."

The old drunk's musings were interrupted by a rumbling belch that Jermaine felt in his core. The bartender set another large mug of Emyhrsen's cheapest ale in front of Melchin, and Jermaine paid another coin, though it pained him to support such a lousy brewery. Everyone in the tavern was drinking the same filth, so he kept his opinions to himself.

"That's the last one I can afford to buy you, friend," Jermaine said. "I appreciate you taking the time to tell me this story, though. Running into you on the road was quite a spot of luck."

"Well, Jerry—"

"Jermaine," he corrected.

"Well, Jermaine, I hope you find what you're looking for"—another belch—"and I'm sorry I can't travel with you. Vulture Hollow is not a place I hit more than once per year, and even then they buy almost nothing from me. Waste of my time, it is. Those cheapskates are quite an unfriendly lot."

"I'll be sure to turn on the old charm, then." Jermaine patted the textile merchant on the shoulder and then made his way outside to his horse.

He wasn't looking forward to even more riding, and he knew his horse was longing for a proper rest, but he felt more and more uneasy with each passing day. He couldn't quite explain it, but his unfounded fear continued to grow. He rode all day, camped under the stars at night, and pressed on again the next morning. He passed farm after farm, as well as the occasional inn, but he hadn't brought enough money with him for a room or a nice meal. King Harold had sent him off with several days' provisions, and he was careful to make them last.

Jermaine set off at the break of dawn on his third day since leaving Elm Springs. At high noon, he passed a painted sign indicating that he was entering Vulture Hollow at last. Other than the incessant cawing of crows and the buzzing of flies, it was unsettlingly quiet. The fields on the outskirts of the town were overgrown, with berries left to rot on the vines. With nobody to chase them off, the birds were making a meal out of just about everything.

A sudden dread washed over Jermaine. He wanted to stop. Turn back. Rush home. Something was not right here at all. But he knew this town would tell him whatever he needed to know before he could return to Ferathan. The truth about the witch would be revealed here.

His horse stopped in the road.

"Come on, old boy," Jermaine said. He pulled on the reins and clicked his tongue, but the horse would not budge. The road continued straight ahead, and Jermaine could see the silhouette of an outcropping of buildings in the distance, so he dismounted and tied the horse to a low, rotting fence on the side of the road. "I guess I'll go it alone, then."

After another hundred feet, Jermaine got his first look at the town. Perhaps *town* was a generous word. It was really just a dozen or so buildings on each side of the main road, a few small shacks farther out, and more farmland beyond. There wasn't a single person in sight.

Jermaine approached the first building and read the sign outside. It was a mercantile shop. He pushed the door open. The place was filled with goods, but there was no proprietor in sight.

"Hello?" Jermaine called. He assumed the owner and his family lived in the apartment upstairs, so he stepped through the doorway behind the counter and called up the stairwell. "Anybody here?"

No answer came, but he was certain he could hear the buzzing of flies above. He turned and rushed out of the shop. The sheriff's office across the road was equally deserted. The bank was empty as well, and it appeared no looters had attempted to make themselves rich. He walked into a restaurant and almost vomited at the smell. He expected to see bodies but found only rotted food on the tables, as if all the diners had left in the middle of their meals and nobody had cleaned up after them. Rats lingered on several of the tables, quite large from their days of undisturbed eating. They didn't bother scurrying away when Jermaine entered; they easily outnumbered him fifty to one.

It was outside the town's only inn that the smell really hit Jermaine hard, and this time he couldn't stop himself from vomiting. This was most definitely not the smell of rotting food.

Every bit of Jermaine, every ounce of self-preservation, wanted to turn around. The hairs on the back of his neck stood up. *Run*, they seemed to tell him. *Run away and never look back.*

But deeper down, he thought of his parents, of Sana, of Gaethen. Ferathan's safety depended on Jermaine. He had to press on.

He approached the double doors of the inn, but they were blocked. Someone had nailed large boards across the doors. He turned to the windows, but they too were boarded up. Jermaine looked farther down the street and saw a blacksmith's shop. He ran over, grabbed the tools he needed, and brought them back to the wretched inn of death. It took a few minutes, but he was able to pry the boards off the door. As he reached for the knob, he glanced down at his feet. Maggots were pouring through the crack at the bottom.

He turned the doorknob and pushed, but something was still blocking the way from the inside. He tried the other door. It was also blocked, but he put his weight into it and forced it.

"No!" he cried as he took in the scene.

Given how many abandoned farms and empty businesses he had passed, plus the shacks beyond the town that he hadn't yet explored, Jermaine had estimated that there must be about a hundred people living in the town. That was about how many bodies were sprawled about in the large great room of the inn. Some were laid out over tables, others hanging off the innkeeper's desk, but most were piled on the floor.

Jermaine ran out and vomited again, but he knew he couldn't give up. He removed his coat and tied it around his mouth and nose to block out as much of the stench of death as he could. Inside, he observed the bodies, trying to understand the cause of death. Some people seemed to have been trampled in a mad rush to escape the inn, but most appeared to have died from a different cause, one he had never seen before. Nearly every corpse had a mark on its face. And even had he known these individuals, he wasn't sure he would have been able to identify them. It was as if their faces had been ...

"Melted?" Jermaine said aloud. "How can this be?"

He bent closer, using all of his self-control not to vomit again, lest he cover his coat in filth and add to the stench in that cursed place. He knelt over a bloated man. The skin seemed to ripple away from the center, as if it had melted, dripped, then dried. There was nothing left of the nose, not even bone. The eye sockets were hollow, but a slimy substance pooled deep inside them. On top of all that, Jermaine thought he recognized a shape that covered most of the face. He turned to another corpse and noticed the same shape.

It was the imprint of a large hand. *A man's hand?* he thought. *It appears as if a man laid a burning hand on each of these people and melted the life right out of them!* He thought back to the witch who had seduced his closest friend. Naliah was quite tall. Perhaps this was not the work of a man at all, but of the towering woman. The witch.

Jermaine's knees gave out, and he fell to the floor between the remains of an elderly woman and a young girl. Despite the reek of death around him, he remained on the ground for several minutes, paralyzed with shock.

Jermaine finally turned his head, finding himself face-to-face with the girl. She reminded him so much of his sister. So much of—

"Sana!" he yelled. He jumped to his feet and ran out the door, leaving it open for the rats and crows and flies to have the feast of their dreams. He darted back up the road to his horse and fell at the animal's feet. He lay there weeping for several minutes, overcome with grief for the people of Vulture Hollow and fear for his family and friends in Ferathan.

And then a shuffling in the cornstalks beyond the fence snapped him out of it.

His first thought was that crows and rats were fighting over prime crops, but then he realized he was hearing footsteps. *Human* footsteps. He stood up but hid himself partially behind his horse.

"Hello?" he called out. The footsteps stopped, and he could see the top of the cornstalks swaying about ten feet away. "Who's out there? Show yourself. I won't hurt you."

Still nothing.

"I just saw what happened in town. I'm sorry. I'm afraid it's going to happen in my own town next. Naliah Lunarra will continue this destruction if I don't stop her."

"Naliah?" The voice sounded like it belonged to a child. "She left us. She left us here, and then they died!"

A little girl came running out of the field.

"Rabia, wait!" It was an older boy this time. He followed her out, and they both came to a halt on the other side of the low fence that separated the crops from the road.

"It's okay, Alex," Rabia said. "He'll help us."

"That's what we thought about the priest, and that's how they all ended up dead," Alex said. He looked to be about fifteen years old, and Jermaine guessed the girl was around five. They were undeniably siblings based on their shared features.

"Did you say something about a priest?" Jermaine asked. "Did he come to help you after that wretched *witch* left?"

"You have it backward," Alex said.

"What do you mean?"

"You say *witch* like it's bad," Rabia said. "Naliah was nothing but kind to us. She didn't do anything. The mean man who chased her away is the bad one."

"Was he a priest of Solendaron?" Jermaine asked.

Alex and Rabia looked at each other uncertainly. "Was he bald with a ridiculous curly mustache?"

"That sounds like him," Alex said. "I think he said his name was Arun. After Naliah escaped, he wanted to make us repent for associating with a witch. He wanted us to follow that sun god of his and beg for forgiveness. He said we had the mark of evil and needed to be cleansed by the fire of Solendaron."

"I saw what happened to the rest of the people here, but how did you escape?"

"I threw up," the girl said.

Her brother reached over and hugged her. "Rabia was sick. A sickness was going around town. A few of the elders died from it not long before Naliah arrived. She was helping us recover when Arun came and chased her off. He called a meeting at the inn, since it was the biggest place for gatherings in town, but Rabia was too sick to go. I stayed home at our farm to take care of her. Our parents never came back after the meeting, but we heard the screams. We hid in the barn and waited for the priest to leave town. We haven't seen anyone since."

Jermaine stood in shock. The man this boy was speaking of had been kind to him, had saved him from certain death when he had plummeted down the hill and into the lake. And Jermaine had sent the man to Ferathan.

Jermaine had sent the man to Ferathan to warn them of the witch.

He had sent a killer to his friends.

These children were the only ones to survive the attack on Vulture Hollow. The only ones who knew how dangerous the priest of Solendaron really was. The only witnesses. Jermaine needed them.

"You must come with me. There is nothing left for you here. Let us gather two more horses and head south."

The next morning, they rode off together to save the people of Ferathan.

Unless it was already too late.

CHAPTER 10

It was as if nothing particularly peculiar or eventful had happened in the small village only three days earlier. The tables and chairs outside of Fielders' Fancies had been cleaned up promptly the morning after the wedding reception. The lawn of the central park was perfectly manicured. The statues stood guard outside Ferathan Manor in the same positions they had always stood. The neighbors took turns delivering hot meals to the house of the newly-weds, whom nobody had seen since, as was customary.

When morning came on the fourth day, Gaethen Devorac opened his front door, completed his morning routine around the farm, and made his way into town for the first time as a married man.

"You can't keep coming to see me in the mornings

now that you're married, Gaethen," Sana teased. She passed a mug of fresh coffee across the counter as she winked at him. "Your new missus ain't feeding you at home?"

"Now, just because I'm married doesn't mean I don't have time to patronize my favorite family's establishment. And no, so far she hasn't done any cooking on account of everyone in town feeding us. We had to start tossing out leftovers for the sheep, we were so overloaded."

"Aye, I *thought* those sheep were looking a bit hefty when it was my family's turn to bring dinner last night. Hope they enjoyed the bread pudding, then."

"There was no way I was letting *that* go to waste!" Gaethen patted his belly. He downed the rest of his coffee and slid the mug back toward Sana. She made to refill it, but Gaethen waved her off. "Best to stop with the one cup. I have to run a few errands around town before I go back to have lunch with my bride."

He noticed something troubled in the woman's stare. He had known her long enough to recognize that look. He raised an eyebrow at her, which prompted her to speak.

"How much of the wedding do you remember, Gaethen?"

"Well, it's not like I was drowning myself in ale! Why wouldn't I remember the most wonderful day of my life? It was quite fun, up until the issue with my lungs. It was the first time I'd felt that way since that night in the caves. Not sure why it happened."

"And what about those statues?" Sana asked.

"Statues?" He passed a coin across the counter to pay for the coffee. "At the manor? Yes, those things are very ugly, but I hardly notice them anymore. They've been there all our lives, and long before we were conceived. Why do you bring them up?"

"Oh, it's nothing," she said.

Gaethen couldn't read her. Was it jealousy she was feeling? He had always known that Sana had feelings for him, but he had always seen her more as a sister than a potential lover. Perhaps she missed her brother or was overworked because of his absence from the brewery. She picked up the coin and the mug and turned away. As Gaethen got to his feet, she spun back around. "You do remember the priest, though, don't you?"

"A priest? In Ferathan? Now, that's a silly thought. What is going on in that mind of yours, Sana?"

She pounded on the counter. "Damn it, Gaethen, you really don't remember a bald man with a huge curling mustache? He was the only stranger at the wedding."

"I can't tell if you're joking. That sounds like a ridiculous-looking person."

"He was one of those sun worshippers. He said he

was from Esteron. I haven't seen him back in town since your reception, but I've heard some folks say he's made camp in the forest along the north road."

"A guest all the way from Esteron at my wedding? Now I feel honored. I didn't think I was *that* special. Are you toying with me?"

Sana let out a frustrated grunt and turned away. She went through the kitchen door without a parting word. Gaethen took out another coin and left it as a tip. It was the best he could do without understanding what was eating at her. Perhaps she *was* jealous after all. Gaethen wished Jermaine were there; he knew how to read his sister better than anyone.

And just where is Jermaine, anyway? Gaethen wondered. *Living it up with the boy king of Emyhrsen?*

🍂

"Sana, dear?"

Sana looked across the kitchen from where she was mashing the grains for what would be a dark, hop-forward brew.

"What's wrong, Mum?"

Geraldine Fielder seemed quite perturbed as she rushed through the maze of barrels. She leaned in, inches from Sana's face, and whispered, "I think there's something going on. Mayor Wylder is here with a very odd stranger, and they've asked to speak with you in private."

Sana immediately knew who the stranger was and what the visitors wanted from her. She gave her mother a reassuring pat on the shoulder. "Don't be concerned, Mum. I'm sure it's nothing. Are they out in the dining room?"

"No, dear. I set them up in the office. I'll take over with the mash. Do you want me to send for your father?"

Sana handed her the long spoon she was using to stir the grains in the boiling water. "No need. I can handle this."

Oh, Gaethen, what will you think of me after this? she thought. *I'm afraid lying in this priest's presence will do no good.*

Mayor Coran Wylder was sitting on the desk in the office. The woman had always taken what she wanted without asking questions. That trait had served her well in her younger years, when she'd first run for mayor. In fact, it was her husband who had originally intended to run unopposed all those decades ago, but the idea of leading the town had been appealing to Coran, so she'd entered the race and beaten her husband quite easily. It wasn't power for power's sake that she thirsted for; Coran had genuinely thought she could bring a lot of positive changes to Ferathan, and she'd made good on that and then some. The town was prosperous; they had a healthy trading relationship with the kingdom of Emyhrsen, relatively good health all around, and no serious crime. It was a safe town, free from outside threats.

At least, until the past couple of weeks.

"Ah, Sana, your mother passed on the message," Mayor Wylder said. She didn't bother getting up from the desk to greet Sana. "From the look of fear on her face, I was afraid she'd take off running with you. Don't worry, though—you're not in any kind of trouble. Do you recognize my friend here?"

Mayor Wylder motioned to the man in one of the chairs in front of the desk. The bald man stood up and bowed his head toward Sana. "A pleasure to see you again, young lady," he said.

"Yes, I remember him from the wedding," Sana said. She looked the man over, grateful for her own sanity's sake that he really existed in the flesh and not just in a clouded dream, but she also dreaded what she expected would come of his presence.

"So, Priest Arun was telling the truth, then," Mayor Wylder said. "I must apologize for putting you to the test, Sana. I have no recollection of his appearance at that fine celebration, but he's told me quite a tale about what went on. Hard to believe a stranger when my own mind tells me his version of events never happened."

"I find it hard to believe myself, if I'm honest with you, Mayor Wylder."

"That's the power of the witch at work," Arun said. "She'll make you believe whatever she wants. She'll put you under her spell and lead you to destruction, if it's to her benefit. That's why I'm here."

"Now, now, dear, the protection of this town is my jurisdiction," the mayor said to him. "I do appreciate your concern for our safety, though."

"Well, I've confirmed that I met our guest here," Sana said, backing slowly toward the door. "If that's all, then I'd best be getting back to brewing. Mother is prone to letting the kettles boil over, and it's a beast to clean up."

"Not quite yet," Arun said. Sana stopped and turned to him. "Will you confirm that you also witnessed an attack by a host of wretched creatures that coincidentally matched those horrendous sculptures at the good mayor's estate?"

"Yes, Sana, for the sake of Ferathan's safety, can you please clarify what you saw? Start from the beginning of the wedding procession."

And so Sana did. With every word she uttered, she felt as if she were tearing a piece of Gaethen's heart away, like a little girl peeling the petals off a rose one by one.

She was sure she knew how this would end.

CHAPTER 11

The moon shone brightly through the windows and into Gaethen's bedroom. It wasn't quite a full moon yet, but near enough to it that Gaethen could see every perfect curve of his new bride's body. He had always been a man of tangible things; he had never spent time dreaming of what he hadn't touched with his own fingers or tasted on his tongue. He had never wasted time thinking about the feel of his skin against that of a hypothetical lover.

Oh, how he'd wasted all those years of his life! There was nothing more wonderful in all the world, as he had learned over the past four days.

Naliah was lying on her stomach, looking at the moon. The glow of that orb in the sky illuminated her red hair like the fire in the hearth. It was a color that always drew Gaethen's eyes in the throes of passion, but it was curiously absent when he closed his eyes and pictured her. In those moments, and in his dreams, he instead saw a woman with hair the color of the moon.

She's right here, he thought to himself, *and her hair is clearly not pale!*

But again, Gaethen only dreamed of things he had seen and knew to be true. So what was this vision that plagued his mind?

"My love, your heart is racing," Naliah said. She turned toward him and pulled her body against his. Again, the feeling was beyond anything he could ever have imagined. "Are you trying to tell me you're ready for it again? If the seed hasn't been planted yet, I don't mind going for another round."

"It's just ..." He wanted with very nearly his whole heart to tell her about those images he could not clear from his mind, but the tiniest part of him knew it would end their first few perfect days together. He wasn't ready to give that up yet. "It's just that some parts of my body aren't quite as quick to recover as my mind is. A few more minutes, perhaps?"

Naliah put her arms around him and kissed him. She pulled back after a few seconds and sat up. If the moon hadn't already done the job, her smile would have lit up the room. "Just think, we may have our own little bundle of joy this time next year. Our own family."

"And a couple of years after that, he'd be big enough to work on the farm with me! I could sure use the extra help."

Naliah lifted her pillow and slammed it into Gaethen's face. "Think again, you big oaf! *She* will live the happy life of a little girl for as long as she needs to. Time is precious; there's no need to rush her into adulthood."

Gaethen laughed and pulled her in for a kiss. "Okay, if you're so sure the baby will be a girl, I guess you're right. But *if* it's a boy, I'm at least going to have him out there shearing those sheep when he's old enough to grip a blade and—"

The creak of the front gate was unmistakable. Gaethen jumped out of bed and reached for his slacks. "Maybe it's one of the beasts coming back for the livestock," he said. He looked to Naliah, expecting fear, but instead saw guilt on her face.

"Gaethen, I—"

"Devorac!" A shout came from outside. Gaethen tightened his belt and pulled on a shirt. He was reaching for his boots when someone pounded on the front door. "Come out peacefully with your wife," the constable yelled.

"I don't know what this is about, but you must get dressed quickly," Gaethen said to Naliah. He tossed

her a dress that was draped over a chair and then
rushed down the hall. When he turned the knob and
pulled the front door open, he started at the sight.

Constable Buckland was alone on the porch, but
at the bottom of the three steps stood Mayor Coran
Wylder, her husband, and a stranger he knew immediately was the priest from Esteron whom Sana had
described. Outside the front gate, nearly half the
town had congregated, including Sana. Many of them
had torches. By the light of the near-full moon and
the flames of the onlookers, Gaethen was quite
certain he could see tears coming from Sana's eyes.

"Gaethen Devorac," Mayor Wylder said before
the constable could get another word out, "I'm sorry
to do this, but we need to take your new bride with
us. There have been some serious accusations against
her, and it's time we sort them out."

Gaethen gripped the door frame with both hands,
lest he lose his balance from the shock. "Naliah? But
... but why? She's been here with me every day since
the wedding. She's done nothing wrong!"

"It's okay, my love," Naliah said. Gaethen turned
to see her approaching from inside the house. In the
windowless hallway, hidden from the light of the
moon and the torches, Gaethen thought he could see
the silhouette of an old hag limping toward him, not
the striking young wife he had been making love with
earlier that night. As she neared the door and entered

the light, however, she looked once again like the woman he knew and loved. She reached up and wiped a tear from his cheek. "I expected this would happen sooner or later, but I had hoped it would be after this baby was born."

"Baby?" Gaethen asked. "What do you mean? How could you know?"

"A woman knows," she answered. "A woman of the Azhelda, anyway."

She leaned in for a kiss, turning his body as she did and positioning herself in the doorway. Then she pulled away from him, turned, and went with the constable without a fight. The mass of townspeople parted to let them pass.

Whatever fireworks the crowd was expecting, they didn't receive them.

Not that night, at least. The full moon was yet to come.

"NALIAH, THE THINGS THEY'RE SAYING ... HOW they could believe that odd man out there ... I don't know what we're going to do!"

Naliah wiped the tears off Gaethen's cheeks with the back of her hand and then stroked his hair. While his eyes were red and swollen from a night of crying and lost sleep, Naliah appeared perfectly composed despite the predicament she was in. At Mayor Wylder's orders, Constable Buckland had allowed Gaethen to visit his wife in her cell that morning as Naliah awaited her impromptu trial.

"The only thing I can do is tell my truth. If they accept it and accept me as I am, than so be it."

"As you are?" Gaethen took a step back from her. "Naliah, that first night you saved me in the cave ... were you the reason I was in that predicament in the first place?"

"Would you love me less if I said yes?"

"And my little black lamb—did you resurrect her? Did you use her to lead me to you?"

"Would that be too grotesque to justify our love?"

"And these glimpses I keep getting of you. Are you as you appear before me now, or is there something else hidden within you?"

"This is why I did not wish to reveal these things to you, but some things are beyond even my ability to hide."

Gaethen backed away more and more with each question until he was pressed against the far wall of the cell. He slid down to sit on the floor. "So, it's true, then? You are what that man says? You are a *witch*?"

Naliah took a step toward him but stopped herself when he flinched. She sat on the floor several feet away from him instead. "I am a sorceress of the

Azhelda. I am not the age I appear to be now. But what's real is—"

"Azhelda? What are the Azhelda?" The terrified look on his face broke Naliah's heart.

"We are from a thousand miles north of here in the icy lands. Where my ancestors lived before that, I cannot say, but I assume they were driven to such a remote place by people who could not accept them for what they were."

"Witches?"

The word seemed to sting her, but she let it go. "We live much longer than the average person if we so choose, but to do so, we must feed off of other sources of life."

"The priest said you've destroyed entire villages. Is that how you stay alive? Is that what Ferathan is— what *I* am—to you? Just another well to sip from on your long journey through this world?"

"No, Gaethen. That's not it at all! *This* is love! *This* is escape from that life, from those people I hail from. *This* is a fresh start and a journey toward a proper end!"

"The only end you'll get now is the end of the rope. They mean to hang you, and I don't know that I can convince them otherwise, or that I *should* convince them otherwise. You do not deny destroying the other places you've passed through?"

"Destruction is what my people were built to

bring about, apparently. I did not ask to be born this way. And it is true that I have ended the lives of many living creatures, but not whole towns full of people. I have used other means."

"The farm animals. Those are what you've been feeding off of?"

"Precisely. It is twofold, though. The Azhelda can certainly feed off of human life. We can consume life in any form. But it's not only killing that works. I've found a method that takes much more effort but works all the same. I can consume life that is still to come. I can stop others from aging and take that stolen time for myself, and when I do, I can also prevent people from experiencing sickness and death. They must be willing, but it can be done. I do not take the lives of other humans, and for that, my own people have cast me out."

"Try telling that to the villages you left behind." Gaethen and Naliah turned to the door, where the newcomer stood. The priest had a devious smile on his face. "The people of Vulture Hollow would disagree if they could. Unfortunately, they are all maggot-infested corpses now."

"They were alive when I left them!" Naliah rose to her feet, but Arun raised his right hand and quickly uttered words in a strange tongue. Naliah flew back against the wall as if launched by an unseen catapult. She crumpled to the floor.

"Try telling that to the people of Moreland Springs. They are bloated from the water they drowned in after you had your way with them." The priest walked across the room to Naliah and spat on her. "Or the people of Decker, had they not already been mauled by whatever predators you unleashed upon them."

"Get away from her!" Gaethen yelled. He climbed to his feet and lunged at the priest, but Arun struck him down without the use of sorcery.

"You know nothing, farm boy. I have followed this wench's trail for years. I have attempted to intervene, to save those she's victimized. She is dangerous, but her time in this world is finally at an end. I'll see to it." With that, Arun turned and walked out of the cell, slamming the door behind him.

Gaethen crawled over to his wife. Blood flowed out of her right ear. Her cheek was purple from slamming against the wall. He held her head in his lap and wept. Despite her pain, she relished in his compassion.

And then the destruction began.

CHAPTER 12

It wasn't the screams that brought Gaethen out of the holding cell behind the constable's office. The ground quaked, and plaster from the ceiling rained down on Gaethen and Naliah. He left her under a sturdy table and went to see what kind of danger they were in. Outside, it was chaos. People were running toward the center of town, nearly plowing him over in their attempt to get away from something unseen.

More rumbling. A pattern. Pounding footsteps.

"Run, Gaethen, it's coming!" Petra Alainy shouted as she sped past him. A large piece of brick siding from a building came flying through the air and smashed down on the woman only a second later. Gaethen stared at the bloody mess in shock until a shadow fell over him. He turned to find an Ogressi towering over him, salivating as if the beast were looking at its next meal. It started to reach its oversize hands toward him when more booming footsteps revealed the presence of another giant. The newcomer tackled the first Ogressi, and they both fell onto the seamstress's shop behind the constable's office. While the monstrous creatures wrestled over which one got to claim Gaethen, he took off running to fetch Naliah.

She was already waiting for him at the door.

"Come on, Naliah, we have to get away from here!"

He reached for her hand, but she refused to take it. "If I run, they will use it against me."

"If you don't run, there will be no more of you left for them to accuse!"

"And that is how they want it, my love." Naliah gestured down the street. "They will blame me for all this madness." Two blocks away, one of the giants was consuming the bottom half of Marsten Hiller. The tanner would never sell his leather goods again. Even at that distance, Gaethen could see the man's insides evacuating the upper half of his body.

A horse-drawn cart flew over a row of buildings and smashed down into the gravel just twenty feet from them, the remains of the animal that had pulled it still attached. Blood splattered onto Naliah. To the east, a fire raged, probably started when the chaos

had made its way to the forges in one of the smiths'
shops. From the west, another giant approached.

"There's no time to worry about what they'll say,
Naliah! We must run!" He grabbed her hand and
started to tug, but she overpowered him and pulled
her hand back. Gaethen fell into the street, and an
Ogressi took advantage of the fall and lunged
forward.

Gaethen closed his eyes, preparing for death, but
death did not come.

A moment later, Gaethen felt hot breath blowing
on him like a wretched moist wind, and he opened
his eyes to find himself face-to-face with the Ogressi.
He slid away on his back, unconcerned with the
gravel scraping his scalp, until he was free. To his
shock, the Ogressi was hovering in the air.

He looked to Naliah, who had her hands held out
toward the beast.

"You see, dear Mayor, Naliah Lunarra has full
control over these beasts," Arun said, arriving on the
scene with Mayor Wylder, Constable Buckland, and
several onlookers. "The only person here she has
chosen to protect is her own lover, and even he is not
safe from harm. Nobody in this town is. She will
destroy you all if you do not execute her
immediately."

Naliah turned toward the priest, but the words
she spoke were not aimed at him. She uttered an

incantation, then pushed at the air. The Ogressi flew across the street and slammed through the butcher's shop, flattening the building.

"But she must stand trial," Buckland said. "That's how we do things in this town. We have rules. Order."

"Order?" Arun asked. "Look around you, my friend. Can a trial really bring order in the midst of the carnage she has brought? The moment life leaves this witch's body, order will come, but not until then. Do what must be done."

"The priest is right," Mayor Wylder said. "I don't like it any more than you, but he is right. All the dark deeds that have happened in this town started with her arrival. That can't be a coincidence. The gallows are ready for her. Let us begin."

"No!" Gaethen yelled. He started to get to his feet when Arun made a small motion with his hand, unseen by the town officials. Gaethen was slammed back to the street by an invisible force. He tried to open his mouth and scream, but no voice came. His lungs were quickly filling with fluid, and he struggled even to breathe.

Constable Buckland approached Naliah. She surrendered once again without a fight.

"I beg you, Constable Buckland, tell me whether the children are safe," Naliah said to her captor as he led her toward the northeast corner of town.

"Aye, they're safe. They were at the school when the destruction started, and they evacuated to the manor. What do you care, though, witch? This is your doing, isn't it?"

Naliah didn't answer. She was relieved that the children had been kept away from the destruction, but there was also fear in her—fear of seeing Gaethen's distraught face. She didn't dare look back at him. Not realizing he was struggling to breathe in the street behind her, she marched on with the constable and the mayor, followed by the crowd.

Chaos continued around Gaethen as he lay dying, but the beasts didn't seem to care about a man at the edge of eternal slumber, and they left him alone. Spoiled meat, he must have seemed to them.

His vision faded as his own lungs drowned him.

Darkness consumed him.

Until it didn't.

"Come ... on ... Gaethen ..." The woman's voice came in spurts between presses on his chest. She put her lips to his, and he knew they weren't those of his lover, but they did belong to one who loved him dearly. He was swimming in blackness, failing to surface in the lake that was his life. With every pump, every breath she put into him, he was lifted closer to the top, but it was not enough.

Now the water that consumed his consciousness did not feel wet, but thick and scratchy. It felt like wool, but it was dark, like the depths of the cave he had nearly died in not long before. But like that fateful night in the cave, he was rescued. The veil was lifted from his eyes; it was the blackness of the lamb his lover had slaughtered and used to ensnare him. And the water consumed him once again.

"Damn it, come on!"

He was moving. Up, up, up. A light. A blessed beam of sunlight, and now he could see. There was a shape beyond the surface. A silhouette. Was it Naliah? He continued moving upward. His head broke the surface of consciousness.

"Sana?" he asked as he gasped for air. He turned and coughed up the fluids that had nearly killed him. "Sana, where is she? Where did they take Naliah?"

He struggled to get to his feet. Sana tried to guide him back down, but he gently pushed her away.

"You must rest," she said. "You don't want to see what they're about to do. There's no stopping them."

"Sana, back at the wedding reception, did you see what she did when I had the attack in my lungs? She could have let me die, but she didn't. She could have let the town perish at the hands of those beasts, but she didn't. I remember now. I remember everything clearly."

"I did see, and I felt the goodness in her. I know it's there. But she's dangerous! So many are dying right now at the hands of the Ogressi she called to attack us. It's her revenge for being arrested."

"She didn't do it! I was with her in the cell when this began. It was that priest. He has some kind of dark powers. We must stop him."

"He said she's destroyed villages, though!"

"No, she used the villages in order to survive, but she did not destroy them. It was Arun who chased her away from those places. It was Arun who did the things he blames her for."

Gaethen saw the look of realization on his friend's face, but he didn't wait for her to admit that she believed him. He took off running toward the estate on the edge of town despite the wheezing in his rattling lungs.

WHEN GAETHEN WAS A CHILD, HIS FATHER HAD created the Farmers' Association of Ferathan. Jensen Devorac had brought together nearly all the crop and livestock producers in the region. They had met up monthly, shared tips and tricks, and found camaraderie with each other. They had organized to demand better rates from their merchants. They had coordinated a weekend farmer's market, where they were able to set their own prices without paying a middleman.

Ferathan had always been an outlier from society. Wedged at the north end of the Forest of Despair, it was too far away from Aepistelle for the kings to lay claim to their lands. To the west, the forest stretched for hundreds of miles until it met the sea, with only the castle of the Vheisenia—whom most people referred to as the Ancient Ones—nestled in a small valley. Those beings had no interest in ruling the Ferathani. The town's nearest neighbors were just fifty or so miles to the north in Emyhrsen, but their kings had always seemed content with Ferathan's independence, which the Ferathani celebrated. It was integral to their culture; they were a stubborn lot.

So it wasn't too surprising when a couple of the farmers in town had declined to join Jensen Devorac's Farmers' Association. Weyla Pullman had been chief among the detractors. She had argued that the dues were akin to taxes, and the town already charged enough of those. She had argued that it was a play for power by Jensen, even though he had never thirsted for such a thing. She had remained independent, negotiating her own contracts and farming in her own way, without the help and advice of the others, and she had prided herself on that.

And then a particularly harsh year had struck. Everyone in town had suffered. A cold front had fallen upon the town in the autumn, ending the harvest early. Animals and crops alike had frozen and died off. By winter, the food stores had been low. The members of the Association had pooled their resources to provide for each other and the rest of the town.

By the start of the new year, Weyla Pullman hadn't been seen for several weeks, but she had declared that she would take care of herself, that she had enough in her stores to make it through. Nobody had seemed too concerned for her, but Jensen couldn't help but feel he had isolated her with his Association. One afternoon, he had braved a freak blizzard and ventured across town to the north-western outskirts. Weyla hadn't answered when he pounded on her front door. He'd decided to check her barn, and that was where he'd found her. Dead. Alone.

The story had always haunted Gaethen's father, and yet, after Jensen's untimely death when Gaethen was a teenager, Gaethen had found himself pulling away from society like Weyla Pullman. The people of Ferathan knew how to look out for each other, though, thanks to Jensen's Association. They hadn't let Gaethen suffer alone. They'd brought meals to him, worked in his fields while he mourned, and helped him get back on his feet as the sole proprietor of the Devorac farm. He'd never been truly alone.

Not like now.

Everyone in town had fled the attacks of the

Ogressi. The giants were still smashing buildings on every block he passed, but there were no people to be seen. They had all run up to Ferathan Manor for protection. Sana was behind him somewhere, perhaps the only other person who wasn't yet inside the walls of the estate. She'd been one of his closest friends for most of his life, but it seemed that now she was against him in her distrust of Naliah. He was alone.

He stumbled down Second Street along the east edge of the park, his wheezing growing louder by the second. He leaned down and coughed out a wad of phlegm that was blocking his throat. A couple of steps later, he collapsed onto the sidewalk from the shortness of breath.

Calm, he told himself. *Breathe in slowly. Breathe out. Focus.*

He pinched a pressure point between his thumb and pointer finger on his left hand and held it for several seconds. It usually helped stop the panic that began every time his wheezing flared up. He coughed again. This time, blood was mixed in with the phlegm. The wheezing got worse, but he had to keep moving. The mayor, the constable, and the priest had Naliah, and they meant to execute her. He had to stop them somehow. He had to save her.

He got back to his feet and looked up. He was face-to-knee with one of the Ogressi. He tipped his head toward the sky to see its face. It reached its right hand down and scooped him up, lifting him until he was at its eye level. Gaethen's heart raced. His lungs attempted to take in more air, but they were clogged. Gaethen coughed up what he could and spat, not trying to hit the Ogressi, though that was unavoidable. His captor seemed to hear Gaethen's struggle to breathe. It sniffed and must have caught the smell of death on him. Instead of consuming Gaethen, the giant merely tossed him over the grass and into a pond.

Cold water overtook Gaethen. It wasn't particularly deep, but in his condition, he couldn't fight its pull. *I'll die here alone*, he thought, *just like Weyla Pullman. Nobody will be there to advocate for Naliah. We're both doomed. This is the end.*

In his last moments, he remembered his childhood: being raised by a wonderful father, being embraced by the Fielder family, and being supported by the townspeople. His brief years of adulthood had been too busy to be lonely, or so he had thought until he'd met Naliah. After she'd come into his life, he hadn't been able to imagine ever living without her. She'd given him the best few days of his life. *What else can top that?* he wondered.

He closed his eyes and let darkness consume him.

By the time Sana Fielder arrived to revive him once more, it was too late.

CHAPTER 13

"People of Ferathan, as destruction rages throughout our town, as our homes and businesses are destroyed by monsters that were called here to harm us, I stand before you to sentence a witch to death," Mayor Coran Wylder said. "She came here to take our lives, but instead, she will give up her own. The crimes she committed against each of us are minimal compared to what she would have done were it not for the brave Arun, priest of Solendaron, who risked his own health and safety to inform us of the true nature of Naliah Lunarra. She is a witch of the Azhelda. She is a parasite who feeds off the lives of others to prolong her own. Well, now her reign of terror will come to an end."

"How do you know she's the evil one?" Calista Sentros yelled.

"Aye, she's walked among us for days and been nothing but lovely," Mr. Fielder called out. "Why believe this strange man?"

Part of the crowd sounded off in agreement, but the majority yelled back.

"Try telling that to my husband and his crew!" Shelby Harpon shouted. "You can't, because they all perished at the hands of the Ogressi on their hunting trip right after that wench showed up in town!"

"And my chickens—all dead," said a farmer. "My crops too. I think the Devorac farm is the one with the least damage. How is that a coincidence?"

Those who opposed the execution lost their courage to disagree any longer. The coincidences were indeed far too great.

In between the grotesque statues, in the center of the path that led up to Ferathan Manor, stood the makeshift gallows that Bernal Wylder and a few of the constable's deputies had hastily constructed that morning. It was there, in the shadow of the castle-like estate, that Naliah Lunarra was thrust forward. Her hands were tied behind her back with a rope. A smaller piece of rope had been tied around her face and between her teeth, preventing her from speaking. Bernal and Deputy Boyd lifted her onto a barrel. They lowered the noose over her head until it hooked under her chin. Arun stepped toward the gallows. While screams and monstrous growls and sounds of destruction rang out from the town behind them, those who were gathered at the manor hushed to hear the priest speak.

"Good citizens, I thank you for welcoming me into your humble town. I am grateful that you have listened to reason. I have long followed the destructive trail of Naliah Lunarra. I have seen the blood and barrenness she has left in her wake. I have failed time and time again to catch up to her and stop her from hurting anyone else. That is, until now. We have done it together. We have captured her, and we will stop her from committing any more evil deeds. You'll see it momentarily when her last breath escapes her body. The killing will stop. The giants will abandon your town. You will rebuild and live better lives than ever before. Solendaron, Lord of the Ever-Giving Sun, Creator of Life and Light, whom I serve with all of my being, will look upon you all with great favor. You will bow down to His greatness once this act is complete and you see what He has done for you. Now, let us finish this."

A low murmuring rippled throughout the crowd at the mention of bowing down to Solendaron. The people of Ferathan had never worshipped any god, and they weren't about to change that.

Arun of Esteron realized this, and he wasted no time in making sure the deed was done. He turned to Naliah and kicked the barrel out from under her.

The wood of the gallows groaned as the rope pulled taut from Naliah's weight. Her strangled breathing was audible despite the gag in her mouth. Her legs flailed wildly but could not gain purchase. As the townspeople looked on, they witnessed a transformation.

Naliah was rapidly aging.

Her red hair faded to gray, then to white. It thinned out before their eyes. Her belly swelled as if she were pregnant, then flattened again in seconds. Her skin suddenly wrinkled and sagged, and she seemed to shrink several inches. No longer was she the young beauty they had all admired. She was something else altogether as she neared death at the end of the rope.

Suddenly, a sound cut through the gasps of the crowd. The hooves of a horse—three horses.

"Stop!" the man on the first horse yelled. "Cut her down from there!"

Jermaine Fielder sped toward the gallows, where the mayor, her husband, the constable, the deputy, and the priest all stood as if to guard the woman hanging behind them. At the last second, all but one jumped out of the way. Jermaine's horse plowed into Bernal Wylder. Jermaine reached out and lifted Naliah as the horse skidded to a stop. With the pressure off her neck, she struggled to draw a slight breath through her collapsing windpipe. He pulled the noose over her head and removed the gag from her mouth.

Jermaine's father and a couple of other men ran up and helped him lower Naliah to the ground. Free from the rope, Naliah began to whisper something that Jermaine could not understand. Before his eyes, some of Naliah's color returned to her ancient skin. She turned over and vomited blood. She got to her knees, then to her feet. She took two steps forward before the crowd heard the footsteps approaching from behind them. One by one, they turned away from Naliah and looked toward the gates of the estate. There was Sana Fielder, struggling to carry a man in her arms.

"It's Gaethen Devorac!" someone yelled.

Several people rushed over to Sana and helped lower Gaethen to the ground.

"He's not breathing!"

"His lungs finally got him this time."

They looked at Sana, who wept but could not speak.

"He's dead!" Mrs. Fielder cried from the other side of the crowd.

"No!" Naliah screamed. She pushed through the crowd in spite of the pain in her aged joints. She reached Gaethen's body and collapsed against him, weeping.

Arun stepped toward Constable Buckland and the

deputy and yelled, "Grab her! Don't let her get away with yet another death!"

They started to make for Naliah, but Jermaine grabbed each of them by the shoulder.

"No, gentlemen. The only murderer in this place is standing right there." Jermaine pointed to the priest.

Arun laughed. "Of course the man is sticking up for his best friend's wife. But blaming a man of the cloth? That's ridiculous, Mr. Fielder. Everyone knows I would not hurt a fly. It would be an abomination to my Lord Solendaron."

"Ask those children, then." Jermaine pointed to the teenage boy and the young girl who had ridden in alongside him. "That is Alex and Rabia Glent of Vulture Hollow. They are the only two survivors after Arun massacred their town. They'll tell you everything you need to know about this evil filth here."

Arun looked at the children with recognition, and the fear on his face was clear to everyone. "Naliah Lunarra corrupted their town! I wanted to wash them clean with the light of the Lord. I tried to get them to repent, to accept His rule, but they refused. I could not let them live on in their evil ways. It was Naliah who corrupted them. Once they rejected Lord Solendaron, only blood would cleanse them. I did what I had to!"

The crowd parted behind Jermaine as Naliah rose

from Gaethen's side and made her way toward Arun. He took one look at the anguish on her face, turned, and started running for the east gate of Ferathan Manor. Naliah lifted her old, gnarled hands as if to cast an incantation upon him, but Sana darted forward and grabbed her by the shoulders.

"Please, Naliah," Sana whispered. "There's been enough death. Don't make them fear you any more than they already do. Let that despicable man run off. He'll find nothing but loneliness and self-destruction."

Naliah turned and faced Sana. They were both grieving the loss of the same man.

"I loved Gaethen," Naliah cried. "I truly loved him. I may have come into this town with the intent of taking what life I could, but when I saw him on that first night, I knew he was someone special. Somehow, I just knew. I wanted to do things right this time. I wanted to be normal, have a family, live a real life, and I could see all of that happening with Gaethen. I didn't want to hurt anyone. I took what I needed to survive; I robbed livestock and even the crops of their essence to prolong my own life, but I never did anything to hurt the people here. It was Arun who caused these attacks against Ferathan." She leaned into Sana and released all of her tears.

Below, the Ogressi were still ravaging the town.

"The armory!" yelled Mayor Wylder from her

husband's side; Bernal was bruised but otherwise uninjured from Jermaine's horse. "We have the old weaponry. We can take the Ogressi down together!"

The people of Ferathan murmured to one another, but no one dared to move. It was Sana who stepped away from Naliah and walked toward the mayor. Jermaine followed. As the mayor led them toward the armory that stood beside the manor, the rest of the town turned and followed suit.

As everyone cleared out, Naliah walked to Gaethen's side and dropped to her knees. She began several different healing incantations she had learned during her hundreds of years of life, but each time, she realized there was no hope. None of them could truly restore a life that had already been lost. She was powerless. She put her head down on Gaethen's lifeless chest and wept.

Light footsteps approached her. Naliah looked up to find Rabia, the young girl from Vulture Hollow, standing over her, Alex not far behind. Rabia put a hand on Naliah's shoulder and spoke. "I'm sorry about your friend."

"As am I. It's not just him I lost, though. He planted a baby inside of me. It grew and died on the vine within while I was hanging up there." Naliah wept some more as Rabia gently ran her fingers through the elderly woman's hair. She wiped away her tears and turned back to the girl. "And I'm sorry about your family and the rest of your town," Naliah said. "I didn't want them to get hurt. I don't want *these* people to get hurt either."

Behind them, the people of Ferathan were emerging from the armory, decked out in mail that didn't properly fit, carrying rusted swords and other decaying weaponry. They were a sorry bunch, but they were doing everything they could to protect what was theirs. Every glare they shot at Naliah seemed to stab into her. She hunched back down to the ground as if in pain.

And then the footsteps approaching her doubled and redoubled. Naliah looked up in spite of the hatred all around her. Coming up behind the adults were all the children of Ferathan. Instead of terror or loathing, the youth looked upon her with sadness and wonder. They walked past their parents and stopped behind Alex and Rabia. Naliah stood tall in front of them.

"There must be something you can do, right?" Rabia asked.

Naliah gazed into the girl's eyes. "You are wise, child. Perhaps you are right. I can do something. I can protect them. I can stop the beasts from ravaging Ferathan. But I must have your horses, and I'm sorry for what you're all about to see."

Alex ran over to where he had tied the horses to a gate. The other children parted to make room as he led the horses to Naliah. She put one hand on each of the animals.

"Turn away, children," she suggested. Most listened, but Alex and Rabia continued to watch as Naliah spoke words in her native tongue. The skin of the horses began to compress, their bones nearly piercing through the tight flesh. At the same time, some of the color returned to Naliah's hair. Her posture straightened. She finished the incantation, removed her hands from the horses, and turned back to the children.

The woman in front of them was not quite as young as the woman Gaethen had fallen in love with, and King Emyhrsen before him, nor was she the old hag who had walked away from the gallows just minutes ago. She was something in between. Behind her, the horses whinnied. Much of their essence seemed to have been removed, but they were alive.

Mayor Wylder led the armed citizens toward the gates where Naliah stood. As much as she had changed, she was still recognizable. Everyone murmured in shock at how the woman had transformed yet again.

"I am sorry for what I had to take from these animals to look this way. It will be the last time I take essence from a life to reverse my aging, but there are other ways I can stay the same age and serve as your protector, if you will allow me to do so. I can end this attack on Ferathan and protect the town, if that is your will, but I'm afraid it will come at a cost."

The ground began to shake as the Ogressi made their way from the outskirts of town toward the manor. The people looked down the hill to find two dozen beasts ready to attack.

"And what is this bargain you would like to make with us?" Mayor Wylder asked.

Naliah looked to Rabia and Alex and the town's youth. Their confidence and trust in her seemed to revive her more than whatever trick she had used with the animals. She turned her attention back to the adults. "I can protect Ferathan from any and all threats. I can keep these Ogressi away from the town. I can keep famine from consuming your crops, stop predators from attacking your livestock. I can shut out unwanted visitors so you'll never again encounter someone like Arun of Esteron who intends to do you harm. But in exchange, I need something to keep my body from aging for the duration of this pact, and I need a place to reside."

"And what exactly is it that you are asking for?" the mayor asked. "No more of your witchy games."

"I am asking for your children—all the children of Ferathan. I will not harm them, but I will prevent them—and all of Ferathan—from aging. I will consume those years for my own preservation as I protect this town. We will need Ferathan Manor.

There, I will reside with the children, whom I will care for as my own. Ferathan will be safe and prosperous. Your children will never age, never get sick, never die under my watch. When my covenant is fulfilled, then the hold will be released, and you can live on as normal."

The beasts were at the gates. They crashed through the low fence, which wasn't designed to keep giants out. Farmers, shopkeepers, housewives, and bakers alike raised their swords and charged at the Ogressi, but they quickly found they were no match for the giants. In mere minutes, they would all be destroyed.

Mayor Wylder turned to Naliah with reluctance.

"You have a deal," she said. "Just put an end to this now!"

Naliah nodded to her, then turned and walked up the path toward the manor. As people screamed in pain behind her, Naliah laid hands on the grotesque statues, one by one. She again whispered in her indecipherable language.

"Everybody get out of the way!" she screamed.

The people turned and saw the odd creatures spring to life for the second time in only a few days. The wretched things lunged for the Ogressi and began to tear the giants apart. It was a bloodbath. Two Ogressi escaped together into the eastern hills known as the Fingers, but the others all lost their lives on the grounds of Ferathan Manor that day. When the last one fell, everyone listened for more chaos in the town below, but there was only silence. They let out a cheer for their safety.

A cheer for Naliah Lunarra.

Under a full moon, they celebrated their new covenant, and the next day, they began to rebuild.

For seventy years, Naliah kept her word and served as their protector. As she had promised, nobody aged during those years. Nobody got sick or died. The crops grew in abundance, and the animals on the farms multiplied. The children remained in Naliah's care, and the town stood undisturbed. Neither Arun nor the Ogressi ever returned to bring harm to the people under the protection of the Witch of Ferathan.

THE STORY CONTINUES

Naliah Lunarra and the children of Ferathan return seventy years later in *Gemma Calvertson and the Forest of Despair*, Book One of the Aepistelle Chronicles. Turn the page to read the first chapter!

Order today on eBook, paperback, and hardcover: https://books2read.com/u/mKwNMZ

A heroine's first adventure. A kingdom's last hope.

Gemma spends her days studying a war her father fought in before her birth, but she realizes that not everything is what it seems. When she sets off to interview an aging hero, she learns about an emerging threat to the kingdom prophesied by the forbidden factions of magic and religion.

Since she can't go to the officials without incriminating her new friend Richard, they must set off together on a journey through an uncanny forest to confirm and neutralize the threat. Can they forge new alliances and defeat the forces of evil without the use of magic or the might of a military?

If they fail, everyone they love will perish.

The Forest of Despair is the first book of the Aepistelle Chronicles, a new series of epic fantasy adventures following an emerging heroine and her team of sidekicks, including a witch with an army of children, a young homeless seer, a giant ogre, a boisterous stage performer, and an all-female crew of pirates.

THE FOREST OF DESPAIR
CHAPTER ONE

It wasn't as if Gemma Calvertson were some sort of *chosen one* foretold by the prophets. Nor did she have any particularly special skills that Abernath knew of, even if she was academically and emotionally intelligent. It was just that she was going to be in the right place at the right time.

Oh, and that wasn't by chance, either.

Abernath had arranged the assignment in secret with Gemma's boss, Garrod Hannon. Sometimes, even evil men can sprout consciences, hoping they bear fruit that make up for their insidious past choices. Abernath and Hannon were two of these men looking for redemption. The girl was a tool for making that happen, even if she didn't know it yet.

Telman Abernath peered over the bannister of the fifth floor of the library, his usual perch as the head of the institution. Unlike many aged libraries, which were dark and dusty affairs, the Royal Library of Aepistelle was a grand place with many windows, including the glass-domed rooftop. There was an open, vaulted space between the mezzanine and the dome above the center of the fifth floor. Thus, natural light could shine upon all corners of the building, especially on the rows of tables that sat on the bottom floor.

That was where the girl, Gemma, sat nearly every afternoon as she engaged in her research. It was where she pored over massive tomes about the taxation rates under one king or another or compared historical accounts of the crown's responses to famines and floods. Maybe the girl did have some kind of superpower after all if she was able to stay awake through all that. Her boss, Hannon, even said that Ms. Calvertson had it in her to become one of the great historians. That is, as long as she stayed within the narrow lanes afforded to her by the latest laws set by King Davin and his Royal Mystic Committee. So much was off-limits these days. So many books burned, so many lies sold as truths, and Abernath himself was regrettably part of it all.

Down below, one of Abernath's assistants handed a note to Gemma. She startled at the interruption, read the note, and turned to look up at Abernath on the fifth floor. Within a minute, the girl had made her way effortlessly to the top of the winding staircase. Abernath opened the half gate that barred unauthorized entry to the library's special collections floor. Up here, there were a number of books that barely made it past the restrictions placed on the Kingdom of Aepistelle over the last twenty-five years, restrictions just older than the girl herself. Some of these books contained limited information on the history and geography of the lands to the north; others were religious texts of some of the less dangerous faiths that had once been practiced in Aepistelle. Even these books had been carefully examined; all had passages redacted, and some were missing entire chapters. Abernath's own hands were responsible for much of it.

"I was told you wanted to see me, Mr. Abernath," Gemma said. She had been up to the fifth floor many times since she had started working for the University Press. It took a request from someone such as Hannon to even be granted access, let alone browse even partially unsupervised. "I don't believe I need anything from the restricted archives today, but thank you."

"Ah, yes, I know, Miss Calvertson. I'll only take a moment of your time." Abernath reached into his deep robe pocket and fiddled with the scroll hidden there. He pulled it halfway out and saw Gemma glance down at it. "I understand you are setting off on a big assignment for Mr. Hannon."

"That's right," Gemma said. "I leave this afternoon."

"Yes, well, my good friend Hannon is very excited about the work you will be undertaking."

Something caught Abernath's eye across the corridor and one floor down. A woman stood at a shelf near the fourth-floor balcony with a book pulled halfway out of place, but she was obviously focusing her attention elsewhere, even if her eyes weren't pointed up at Abernath and Gemma.

What a fool I am, standing here in the open while I incriminate the girl, Abernath thought. *They're already on to me—and on to her—and I haven't even given her the scroll.*

"Is there something wrong, Mr. Abernath?" Gemma asked.

Abernath shook off his thoughts, but the expression on his face was grave. He tried to force a smile as he shoved the scroll back down into his pocket, then wiped his brow with his empty hand.

"Uh, no, I'm sorry. An old man's mind isn't always the sharpest, even when surrounded by a lifetime of books. I just wanted to wish you good luck on your journey, and we look forward to seeing you take up your favorite seat in the study room when you're back."

"Oh, okay, thanks, Mr. Abernath. I should be seeing you again in a couple of weeks. Take care!"

The girl flashed a genuine smile at the old librarian, then went back through the gate and down the stairs to where her books awaited her.

Abernath looked back down to the fourth floor, but the strange woman was gone, and the book she'd been touching was still halfway out of its place on the shelf. The slight creak of the gate sounded, and Abernath turned toward it.

"I'm looking for the section on treason against the crown," the woman said.

Abernath was taken aback. *How could the Royal Mystic Committee know about the plan?*

"I'm sorry, but you must have a referral to be up here," Abernath said. Despite his years as the head of the library, he had never developed a voice of authority.

"I think you know of my commander, don't you, Mr. Abernath?" The woman walked slowly toward the librarian as he stepped backward. "I believe you know of Sir Marin Allemon and the Royal Mystic Committee. Is that enough of a referral?"

"There must be a mistake. We do not have any books of interest to you here."

Abernath's hand crept back into his robe pocket as he backed into the bannister. He could just make out Gemma down below, gathering her materials and preparing to leave.

"I didn't say anything about a book, you fool. It's a scroll I'm looking for."

The woman reached under her coat and pulled out a throwing dagger. At the same time, Abernath pulled his hand out of his robe. The scroll in his possession wielded much more power than the woman's weapon.

He reached over the railing and dropped it at the same moment the woman released the dagger. Abernath slumped down against the banister, blade protruding from his left eye, as the scroll plummeted down through the sunlit rotunda. With his one remaining eye, Abernath watched as the rolled-up parchment landed on the marble floor just behind Gemma Calvertson.

The girl did not seem to notice.

Abernath's mission appeared to have failed.

The heavy double doors on the first floor flew open. An unnatural gust of wind stormed the library. Books flew off shelves, papers scattered from the study tables, and patrons jumped to their feet in surprise. Abernath noticed that his attacker seemed to forget about him, and he managed to push away from her to get a better look.

He heard the sounds before he saw what made them. From the front door, from the unlit fireplaces throughout the building, and crashing through the domed windows above, thousands of pigeons swooped in and circled the library frantically. Abernath could just make out a figure emerging from among birds at the front entrance. It was a strikingly tall man.

"What sorcery is this, Abernath?" The woman from the Committee slammed her boot down onto the librarian's left kneecap.

Abernath cried out in pain. His attacker lifted her foot and was about to hammer it down on the same spot once again when she was pushed off balance by a swarm of pigeons. She screamed as she fell on the floor next to Abernath and flailed her arms and legs at the birds.

Abernath looked back down to where Gemma was collecting her scattered papers from the floor. In the pile, unbeknownst to the girl, was the scroll. Abernath watched as Gemma hastily shoved everything into her bag. As she rose, ready to flee, the mysterious tall man set his hand on Gemma's shoulder and appeared to speak a few words. The girl froze for a moment before walking calmly out the front doors of the library.

The blood was overtaking Abernath's vision when he spotted the tall man again, now just a few feet away at the top of the stairs. Up close, Abernath could clearly see his features and chuckled, perhaps too joyously for a man in the last moments of his life. The newcomer was hairless but for the comically large handlebar mustache protruding from his face. He was dressed in a fine suit. He was, Abernath recognized, a priest of Solendaron. And if a clergyman of one of the long-outlawed religions was making such a bold attack in Capital City, then perhaps redemption truly was close.

Abernath's remaining eye closed for good, but his other senses still worked for a few more moments. He heard the woman screaming, felt the wind created by the birds flying all around, and then the screams again, seemingly descending through the air to the marble floor below. He felt a warm hand on his shoulder, and a man's voice spoke softly to him.

"The girl will succeed," the priest of Solendaron said to Abernath as the librarian took his final breath. "You may rest now, my friend, for the girl *will* succeed."

Please join my email newsletter for free content and exclusive announcements at https://www.ryanhoytauthor.com/newsletter.

Gemma Calvertson and the Forest of Despair - Book One of the Aepistelle Chronicles

Freddy Goodman (Ain't No Goodman) - A short story

Raventree Hollow - A gothic horror tale coming in 2022

ACKNOWLEDGMENTS

Thank you, dear readers. I hope you enjoyed this and are looking forward to more great stories ahead, both in the world of Aepistelle and also in new worlds.

Thank you to my family for supporting me on this journey, especially my wife Marsha and our daughters Natalie and Daisy.

Thanks also to my writing buddy Muriel Tronc for reading early versions of my stories and providing invaluable feedback. Please seek out Muriel's young adult thriller, *Five More Pixs*, and her follow-up, *Call Me, Gwapo*.

Thanks to Gabriella Regina for the beautiful cover design, and to Randy Laybourne for creating my publishing logo.

There are many more stories to come. Thank you for coming along with me on this journey.